A Farewell to the Earth and Kepler-438b:

A Noveramatry

A combination of novel, drama and poetry

all in one line

Affectionately dedicated to

UUU
U
U
UUU

who believe there is no skin between us

Mehdi Ghasemi

A Farewell to the Earth and Kepler-438b:

A Noveramatry

A combination of novel, drama and poetry

all in one line

A Farewell to the Earth and Kepler-438b: A Noveramatry
(A combination of novel, drama and poetry all in one line)

Text Copyright © 2019 by Mehdi Ghasemi

Cover and interior design: Mehdi Ghasemi

Front cover photo: Pixabay License

Publisher: BoD™ – Books on Demand, Helsinki, Finland
Manufacturer: Books on Demand GmbH, Norderstedt, Germany

ISBN: **9789528020486**

Con10ts

List of Correctors and Corrupters:

Captain

Co-pilot

Allan Carter

Alex Hewson

Barron Whiteman

Loudspeaker

Alice Walton

Doctor

Someone; Later Kim Atwood

Andy Weir

Somebody

Philip Windsor

Emma McCain

Wilhelm Miller

NASA

Captain Jr.

Setting

Area: T.here

Era: Then

Orbit 10

P.ass.engers

Captain

This is your captain speaking. Welcome to Flight 111, non-stop to Kepler-438b. The distance between the departure point and destination is 640 light years. Fortunately, the atmospheric condition is calm, and let's hope for a smooth and uneventful flight. The temperature in the destination is now 27 °C, which is equal to the temperature of the good olden times of the earth. Please sit back, fasten your seatbelt, relax and do not forget to take your nutrition capsules on time. I provide you with more information during this non-return journey. On behalf of myself and the Co-pilot, I wish you a pleasant flight.

Allan Carter cast a sidelong glance at pass.engers around himself to see how they feel. The spacesuit and equipment attached to his body had made it inconvenient for him to move his head. Stress was k.illing him.

Allan Carter

What would happen to us? It's a non-return journey! Will we die? Will we survive? No one knew!

After a month of intensive courses and exercises, the passengers on board had been prepared for this one-way journey to Kepler-438b. The 100 passengers on this particular spaceship were all famous affluent tycoons, athletes, scientists or politicians who had found the earth no longer habitable and heritable, and as the last resort, they left all their fame and name, companies and properties behind just to save their own lives.

According to NASA, among all other celestial planets, Kepler-438b owned some similar features to the earth. Both had roughly the same amount of land surface area as well as sustained polar caps, and both owned a similar tilt in their rotational axes, affording strong seasonal variability. Like the earth, Kepler-438b had undergone some levels of climate change in the past; however, since it orbited in a habitable zone, its temperature believed to be neither too hot nor too cold for man. NASA though discovered that the radiation emitted from Kepler-438b was more than the earth, and this would make life for man improbable.

Allan quickly reviewed what had happened during the last ten years, which had put the earth in such a desolate state. Deforestation set off a series of changes in climate patterns and negatively affected life glocally. Global warming made some parts of the world inhabitable, and thus, residents of those areas moved toward some parts in the US and Canada. Water crisis, drought and famine in some parts of Africa, Asia and South America k.illed some people, caused some local conflicts and wars and enhanced forced migration. Flood and earthquakes jeopardized the lives of many people and left some people homeless. Political crises between countries, their inability to solve their concerns through negotiations and their resort to revenge and sanction in lieu of dialogue opened the gate for further violent confrontations. Religious superiority in the Middle East passed the zenith and resulted in direct clashes. The climax of all these 10sions was the Third World War that in10sified the situation.

To earn money, they sold weapons of mass destruction to some countries with no control, and then to sell more weapons and earn more money, they added fuel to the fire of national biases, religious superiority, political dominance and differences of any type among countries. Several countries had turned to arsenals for WMD in the Middle East, and they no longer needed to purchase weapons. Then, they caused some wars so that those countries use some of their stored weapons and order more weapons, but they failed to foresee that this conflagration spread rapidly to their own realms. Many countries, directly and indirectly, were entangled in that deadly war that lasted for years and made many areas inhabitable, forcing many civilians to move to the US and Canada. Consequently, billions of people desperately left their homes, and no wall, police or army could stop their mass movement. It was as if starving grasshoppers had attacked the plantations, and nothing could hinder them.

They dashed towards supermarkets, department stores and fast foods in large numbers and gobbled their edibles, and security guards and police officers were unable to threaten, arrest or stop them. Tear gases were less effective than any time. Their hungry bellies had no eyes to shed tears. Some of them scrambled for shelter. They cut the trees in national parks or forests to build some cabins for themselves, while some others occupied houses of Americans and Canadians. This caused lots of brutal quarrels and bloody fights, and some people from both sides lost their lives. There was no amount of order, since millions of homeless people were living in public areas, such as streets, lanes, airports, libraries and train stations, blocking driveways and public transportations. Some of them who had just come back from a heist used to perform their religious rites together in streets. Their presence had made order absent!

There was no amount of protection, either, since armed burglaries and highway robberies recurred every second, and shopping centers were waylaid in light in peace in presence of security guards. Allan recollected a punchy video wherein some hungry angry men with tattered and torn dresses, unkempt hairs and naked feet dashed into a department store to grab some foodstuff and mercilessly killed a store clerk, who resisted. The hands of the man who killed the clerk left red marks on foodstuff he hurriedly put in big plastic bags. To die or to kill, that was the question!

Liquidated in scarlet flood
Hand stained with blood
Dagger embarrassed in flush
Food painted in bad blush
flush & blush
relish & reddish
flood & blood
Who is sued
for bloody food?
Who is to blame?
Who made this flame?

As a result, many businesses suspended their activities. Fire and fury, smoke and scream, shots and shouts, dust and destruction, blast and blood blended, lamed and flamed all living creatures. Death was closer than any time to anyone at any given moment. To save their lives, people were cautioned to stay at home, but home was not sweet and safe anymore. Any moment burglars could break in, murder the owners and occupy it.

The governments of those countries lost their control over their territories. Thousands of prisoners, criminals and murderers absconded from the prisons and joined the havoc. Due to language barrier, it was impossible to communicate with newly arrived immigrants. Some people committed suicide. All of a sudden, Allan stood up and sang out as loud as he could roar:

Allan
Why? You idiots destroyed the earth! You are responsible for this horrible condition. You only thought of your own profit, and now we have to leave the earth. Hey Alex Hewson! You fucked the earth. You made us homeless! Now enjoy your money, your mansions, your hotels, your pools, your authority, you son of a bitch!

Alex Hewson
Me!? Only me?! All these people should be blamed. How can you purge yourself of any guilt?

Allan
Don't blame me! Not me at least! I produced electric cars to save the earth. So cross my name out from your list!

Alex
Are you kidding me?! Did you even think where did the body of your cars come from? Did you even think how electricity was

produced for your cars? Did you care about the environment or your own pocket, and if the environment, why did your cars cost an arm and a leg? Who could afford to buy them? Do you think we were born yesterday?

Suddenly a man furiously shouted:

Barron Whiteman
Shut up! We make Kepler-438b great, even better than the earth. So forget about the earth.

Allan
Your fucking dad did America great. Enough is enough, idiot!

Captain
Well, it's me again, your captain. Please keep silence. We will fly in 10 seconds. The countdown starts now.

Loudspeaker

10

9

8

7

6

Allan lOOked around. He could detect anxiety in the face of his companies who were escaping the mess they had made. Allan's h.ear.t beat so loud that he could h.ear it in his ears.

5

4

3

2

1

Alex
Barron

The spaceship suddenly ejected. An uproar was heard. That was no longer a simulation that they had experienced in their trainings in NASA. That was a real one. They were flying to an unknown desti.nation. It seemed like the journey of death, which is still totally unknown to man, and no one knows what would happen to us after death! No one knows what would happen to others after the death of the earth, either!

To increase its longevity, the spaceship did its best to repel gravity with no levity. After some sudden bumps and rumbles, which stroke fears in the hearts of all passengers, the spaceship finally became smooth. Allan took a deep breath and wiped the sweat from his forehead.

Allan
What is waiting for us? Do we even reach that unknown destination, or the spaceship just blows up midway? I don't wanna run out of life here.

Alice Walton
My heart says that we won't make it. I mean, we all die soon in the space with no grave and gravestone! We just preponed, and *not* prevent, our death time! Death in Space!

Allan
Did you hear what I thought?

Alice
Of course! If I could not hear what others think, how could I maintain being the richest family in the US?

Allan
So you think we all die here?

Alice replied in low and awe:

Alice
Yes!

Sweat was running down Allan's armpits, while his throat was dry. Alice's faint prediction sent a shiver to Allen's frame from top to toe. He wished that he could sip some wine to wash away his fear and anxiety that was k.illing him, but he had only some capsules and a little water. Nothing else! He cleared his throat.

Allan
So what?! What do you have from that maintained wealth now, lady? We all lost everything! We all had very big dreams, but we made them so BIG that finally it burst. Now we are plagued by a nightmare. We are losers, aren't we?

Alice
True!

The spaceship was on its way smoothly. The passengers were more or less quiet. Perhaps they were all thinking about the name and fame, welfare and affairs that they had left behind. What they had troubled to achieve fell apart just like a spider's cobweb! What a nasty life! What an unlucky generation we were! Allan wished he had been born 100 years earlier and used all his potentials to stop the trend that ruined both the earth and his earthly life!

In her spacesuit, Alice felt that she had been mummified alive or rather had been located in a coffin alive; however, it was not clear how long this would b.last. Will their spaceship explode soon? Will they hit a planet on the way? Is their spacecraft hit by micrometeorites? Will they be suffocated due to lack of air? Will they die because of the lack of food? And if they land on Kepler-438b, which is impossible, how long would they survive on that planet? Are there *other* unidentified living creatures there, or are they the first ones who set foot on it?

Sometimes we have to risk, and those, who do not dare to risk, gain nothing. However, those, who make risks, sometimes lose everything! Alice pondered.

Allan
You're right!

Alice
Did you hear my thoughts?!

Allan
Yes!

Alice
How is it possible? It seems that our thoughts are echoed here. So we should govern our mentality here! It's not like the earth that we could hide our thoughts!

Allan
Alice
Allan

Captain
This is your captain again. I hope that you have already had a pleasant journey. From now on, you can have some exercises. There are two treadmills at the very end of spaceship for passengers of third class. There are also two treadmills for passengers of second class, and two for first-class passengers in their own sections. They should be used in turn, as you have been instructed in

the courses. When the light above your head is green, you can slowly walk to the treadmills and use them. Enjoy!

Alice

Useless, isn't it? How optimist the Captain is. He thinks we survive!

Allan

What else can he do? And what else can we do? Let's enjoy at least the last moments of our lives!

Alice

How can we enjoy when our hearts are pressed hard?

Allan

Just think that we are lucky who could escape the earth. Now that we are talking together, many people are losing their lives on the earth, and if not, they die soon. We have been granted another chance to live that they no longer have. I am anxious just like you, but what other choice do we have?

Alice

Do you mean forced choice? I remember the opening words of Charles Dickens' *A Tale of Two Cities*. Have you read the novel?

Allan

No!

Then, Alice began to recite the opening words by heart:

Alice

It was the best of times, it was . . . the worst of times, it was the age of . . . wisdom, it was the age of foolishness, it was the epoch of belief, it was the epoch of . . . incredulity, it was the season of light, it was the season of . . . darkness, it was the spring of . . . hope, it was the winter of despair, eh, I forgot it. . . . . yes, we had everything before us, we had nothing before us, we were all going direct to heaven, we were all going direct the other way.

But despite all these, yes, as you said, let's think that . . . we are
the *luckiest*!

Allan
Not the *luckiest*, since in the spaceship, we are among the third-
class passengers. In front of us, there are 10 first-class passengers
and 30 second-class ones. Two treadmills for 10 people, two
treadmills for 30 second-class passengers, and two for 60 *other*
passengers! They also have extra capsules of oxygen and packs of
nutrition capsules and some extra water bottles.

Alice
Right! This nasty class has always been and will be as long as
mankind lives! They are more human than us. We are ordinary;
they are extra-ordinary.

Allan
This reminds me of *Titanic*.

Alice
While on the earth, we also enjoyed our race and class superiority.
Remember?! Good old days are over! Anyway, we have no phone
or computer to play a game, no TV to watch a movie and even no
book to read. How tedious life in space is!

Allan
Right, and even if we get there how can we survive without these
devices? While on the earth, I could not live without my cell phone
even for 10 minutes!

Alice
Me too! I could live without food for one day but could not live
without internet even for a second. I hope that there will be some
movies on board as we were told in the training courses.

Before long, the lights were green for Alice and Allan to com-

mence their exercises. They stood up and moved one after the other toward the treadmills. Suddenly, there happened some severe turbulence.

Alice and Allen fell down.

The continuous turbulences made passengers scream insanely.

Captain
This is the Captain speaking. Please keep calm. We are entering a new orbit, and such occasional turbulences are quite unpredictable. Stay where you are until orbit transition is over. We anticipate reaching stability again soon.

Alice and Allen sat up!

Alice
Really?! I'm afraid. It seems that our ship is in peril of a fatal tempest.

Allan
Don't worry! Let's count to 10 together. Are you ready?

Allan hugged Alice and started counting:

AliceAllan
1, 2, 3, 4, 5, 6, 7, 8, 9, 10

Soon the turbulences faded away.

Alice
Thanks Allan for your support. How many of these orbits do we have ahead of ourselves?

Allan
No idea!

Orbit 9

Ration the Nation

The agony had gone, and the scream had ceased. Allan and Alice moved toward the treadmills in di.stress. They expected to experience the same severe turbulences anew. Allan's cheeks were as red as blood, and Alice's eyes were bloodshot. No one could help them at this stage, save themselves. Allan cleared his throat.

Allan
Welcome to the new orbit, Alice!

Alice
Thank you for your warm welcome!

They both giggled but a giggle full of trauma. On the way toward the treadmills, Allen cast a lOOk at some passengers. Some pre10ded to be asleep and some l0oked pale, while some were having a quiet chitchat with their family members or fellow passengers. Allan was confident that all passengers in all classes had one common concern, and that was survival. He now could understand some of the concerns of immigrants who desperately left their homes, took on a small boat and were on water for months. Now he could understand them and the true value of life.

The best way for Alice to skip such a trauma was to fall asleep. While in prosperity, she always asked herself why some people commit suicide and put a dot at the end of their life sentence? Now she understands! They had nothing to do, nothing to love, nothing to enjoy and nothing to care. Through sleep, she could not understand how time and spaceship fly. Sleep is the death's twin brother, she thought. So her sleep could also be an introduction for her death, and if not, she did not need to live with such a trauma for the rest of her restless life.

She could remember her time of glory. Tens of reporters and cameramen were always waiting for her to leave her house, and as soon as she appeared, they rushed to have a word with her and take numerous photos of her in a second. Within ten minutes, numerous newspapers, magazines and TV channels reflected her words and works. They knew how to make long sentences out of a single word she had uttered. She used to nag that she had no privacy and did not know how to avoid those distractors. But now, there is no reporter or journalist to talk to her, and no photographer to record the moment of her death or inform her fans of her death! She was dead. How much she had tried to build up that level of global fame and fortune for herself, but where is it now? Gone, yes gone!

If she knew that all her fame and fortune, wealth and health would die untimely, she perhaps did not trouble herself, and instead, she lived a life for her own. No time to regret. She decided to clear her mind. She looked at Allan. He had also closed his eyes. She closed her eyes, too. Silence reigned! It was as if the whole spaceship was dead. Silence - - - - - - - - - -

Captain
Allan
Alex
Barron
Loudspeaker
Alice
Somebody
Emma

However, silence and peace did not last long. It was the calm before the storm. Severe turbulences, more severe than previous ones, broke the silence of the passengers who just screamed in frenzy! Among all screams, Alice could hear the low-pitched wail of an infant.

Captain
This is your captain. It appears that a massive fiery meteorite is fast approaching us. I try to detour as fast as I can to avoid any accident, but stay in your seats, fasten your belts and act based on the instructions you received in the courses to minimize any possible damage.

Minimize the damage?! If the meteorite hits us, we all die, Allan thought. So how can we minimize the danger? It is a matter of life and death, to be or not to be, and not minimizing or maximizing, that's all!

Alice
That's right!

Allan
Did you hear my thoughts again?!

Alice
Yes!

The spaceship received sudden shakes. Alice could feel her heart in her mouth. It seemed that the Captain was doing his best to save the spaceship. No doubt, the Captain was himself a passenger, and they were all in one boat, or rather in one spaceship. The spaceship had become a small boat enmeshed in heavy storms with no control. Passengers' loud screeches had further in10sified the situation. Allan hoped he had not been alive witnessing such a dreadful atmosphere. Something said that this is the end, and it was. Alice was right! Eventually, the meteorite hit the spaceship and smashed it. All passengers lost their lives immediately.

Allan's loud scream suddenly awakened Alice.

Alice
What's wrong?! Keep calm Allan. Were you dreaming?

He opened his eyes. It was as if he had been reborn. Allan gazed down at Alice, overwhelmed with the joy of life!

Barron
Hey you! Keep your voice down! Why do you scream like a woman?

Alice
You don't stop sexism even at the death point?

Barron
Death point?! What are you talking about? I never die. Death is just a delusion. I am only thinking about building towers, skyscrapers, golf courses and tennis courts on Kepler-438b!

Allan
Barron

Allan
Alice, are we still alive?

Alice
Physically yes!

Allan
Alice
Allan

Alice, however, was thinking of survival. She had heard that there exists a goddess, called Fortuna, who has a wheel. People are located around her wheel; some are on top, some on the sides, while some *others* stand at the bottom of it. Every now and then, Fortuna turns the wheel based on her will, and that changes the positions of people. Accordingly, a king is toppled down, and a poor man ascends to the throne! Alice would never imagine that this happens to her. She always thought that she would be in power for good!

Captain
Captain again. It is time to have your first nutrition capsule. Carefully take a deep breath, detach your oxygen masks, sip some water, have your capsules, sip some more water and finally attach your oxygen masks again. Remember that you have only a bottle of water for the whole journey until we land on Kepler-438b. So try to ration it as practiced.

Alice had a horrible feeling. She recalled how she ordered to change the water of her swimming pools over and over again, but now she had no access to enough water even for drinking! Who is responsible for this? FORTUNA or US? Do we destine our destiny with our decisions and deeds, or Fortuna does it for us? She had no idea!

Allan
I have really missed my regular five-course lunch in Ten Madison
Park with lots of food diversity, beverages, desserts and live mu-
sic.

Alice
Me, too, but for now we should enjoy these small capsules!

Allan
For now or for ever?

Alice
For now as I do not think any ever exists.

Allan
Alice
Allan
Alice

The energizer capsules and the spaceship's smooth flight had
brought back peace of mind to some passengers. To provide more
peace of mind to passengers, the spaceship designers had decided
to install no windows in the cabin, and thus, the Captain and the
Co-pilot were the only ones who could see the outside universe,
galaxies and planets.

Sometimes, Alex felt like being in a coffin, carried by an ambu-
lance, heading for a cemetery. Sometimes, he felt like being in a
submarine under the ocean, drowned but dived lived, and sometimes he felt to be on Noah's Ark! Like other passengers, Alex was
curious to learn about the latest news of the earth and his own
properties, but lack of connection to the earth or media had made it
but impossible.

He felt like a dead man, totally disconnected from the earthly world, entangled in a mass grave with hundreds of other buddies. He remembered the live red worms, which he packed in a tiny box and used as baits for fishing. How did the hapless worms feel? he quest.ioned himself. Then, he regretted how he killed a worm to kill a fish just for his own ephemeral joy.

Despite the regular use of the treadmills, Allan had some back-ache. Like other passengers, he had to sleep in a sitting position. Due to prolonged sitting for long, he could feel the heavy pressures of his spine on his lumbar disc. The spacesuit has made his condition even worse. Who could imagine such a tense condition? He wanted to shout as he used to do at his secretaries and employees, but a quick glance at Alice's pale face turned his at10tion to her.

Allan
Are you okay?

Alice did not reply.

Allan
Alice, are you okay?

She did not reply! Perhaps she was sleeping like a log, or perhaps she had died. What shall he do? He had no idea!

After a slight he   sit   a   tion, he touched her wrist.

Allan
What has happened to Al.ice? Why is she cold?!

Desperately, he shook her shoulder, but still she showed no reaction to the jerky movements.

Voice, come out of the silence!

        Breath, come out of her mouth!

                Ocean, show a rapid motion!

A feeling of panic grew in Allan and made him press the emergency button above his head.

Captain
Yes!

Allan
The passenger . . . next to me seems to be . . . . . dead. She looks pale . . . . and does not move at all!

Captain
Thanks for the notification. We take action right away!

Panic bubbled within Allan. He could not take his eyes off Alice. He fixed his eyes on her eyelids and tried to detect some slight moves in them, but her eyelids seemed to be frozen.

Doctor
What'z wrong?

The Doctor talked lispingly!

Allan
I don't know! She looked abnormally pale. At first, I thought she is asleep, but then I detected some end-of-life symptoms.

Doctor
Let'z zee!

The Doctor began some examinations; however, his spacesuit had made it hard for him to do the examinations quickly. After some quick examinations, he brought a new oxygen capsule, attached it to her mouth and continued his job. This made the passengers around feel more worried.

Allan
What has happened to her?

Doctor
Doctor
Doctor

Allan
Why are you silent? Say something!

The Doctor's long silence gave Allan and other passengers around the heebie-jeebies.

Orbit 8

No Space in Space

Allan and his other fellows soon lost one of their fellows. As the Doctor finally stated, Alice had a heart attack because of excessive di.stress! Allan was sad to lose not only a good company but also a potential beloved. How fragile we are, but our pride and prejudice have deafened the ears of the world. Allan always believed that they all die together in one single moment, an anonymous death, but he was dead wrong! Nevertheless, how could he stand a dead buddy sitting next to him for the rest of the journey, but she seemed to be a sleeper.

They buried Alice in a sitting posture. When the coffin is the space, the funeral is the universe! She was no longer earthly, but heavenly! Every now and then, Allan cast a furtive glance at Alice's pale face. A sweet smile on her peaceful face showed that she was con10ted with her own personal journey. Was Alice in wonderland? Allan had been panicked! He used to faint at the sight of blood, and he could not imagine that one day he would sit next to a dead buddy for an unlimited period of time!

Allan
Oh my God! When does this nasty journey end? When does this nasty life end?

Allan heard some wailing from the other side of the spaceship. He was curious to know what was happening over there, but he could not move. Desolately, he sharpened his ears to find about the causes of wailings. He used his ears to see, and his eyes to h.ear. After a lot of struggle, he found that a kid had lost her life, too, and her parents were wailing. How long could this continue? It seemed that the fall time in the spaceship had commenced, and passengers were falling one after the other.

Right after her death, Alice met a homeless person with long unkempt hair and rip-off dirty clothes. It was hard for Alice to detect whether s|he was he or she. Alice turned her head to avoid any possible eye contact with him|her; however, s|he called Alice by name.

Alice was bewildered!

Alice
Who are you?

Alice
Alice
Alice

Alice
GOD?! Are you God?! Oh my God! How is it possible? The whole universe is yours! Millions of churches, mosques, temples and synagogues are yours! So why are you homeless?! Why . . .

God sighed and covered her|his head with his|her old brown blanket. S|he seemed to be hungry and thirsty; thirst and hunger for more at10tion. Alice addressed him|her again, this time with awe:

Alice
Why don't you stop all these adversities and adversaries on the earth? Wars, assaults, hunger, inequality, poverty, natural disasters, depressions, discriminations, droughts, diseases, deaths, killings?

While Alice was thinking that God had no power to change even her|his own conditions, God was thinking that "YOU are responsible for such calamities; you forgot me; you denied me; you ignored the wisdom I offered for your thriving life. Rather, you only thought of wealth and ownership in any possible and impossible way; you destroyed the nature, killed animals and other human beings just to achieve superiority, and now you ask me to stop the adversities and adversaries that you have made!? I granted you wisdom, but you thought of your own kingdom!

Allan thought that he would be the next leaf to fall. This pressed his heart hard. He wished he had not taken this journey. As he knew, there were thousands of selected rich and famous volunteers in line to take this journey. He wished he could warn them of the horrible consequences of such a journey that would only prepone their death. He felt like a dead person with no connection to the living ones.

While younger, he was curious about life after death and wished to meet a dead person to ask whether there was any life after death, but now he had been entangled in life after earth. He was always suspicious of the existence of any life after death and believed that such beliefs had been presented to control mankind; otherwise, we all die and decay. If they manage to land on Kepler-438b, will they die and decay, too? Will their bodies function as it did on the earth, or will they lead an eternal life there? He had millions of questions in mind, but for the time being, he wished he had a company.

Lonely he was,

What was the cause?

Where were his cars?

He pressed his jaws.

Men, we all make mess,

We brought earth distress

We failed to truly profess

Harms we did to earth

for our own race and success

Now we all shall say "bye"

To all plants we made dry

Let us now publicly decry

We killed the earth and the sky

Captain

This is the Captain speaking. We are preparing for landing. Please have another nutrition capsule. By now, you should have drunk one bottle of water. We will distribute some more water among you after landing, but we all should take a good care of water and capsules. We will need them to survive for a while on the Kepler-438b until we find a sustainable way for survival. But for now, please remain seated and keep your seat belts fastened. While approaching and landing on Kepler-438b, we might receive an unexpected welcome from it, so be well prepared!

After hearing the Captain's words, Alex, just like other passengers, was both excited and stressed; sad and happy; a mixed feeling! They were going to land after lots of tension, stress and indeterminacy. However, he was not sure if Kepler-438b lets them land! What was waiting for them? He thought! He had no idea whether they would find water and life there. They just wanted to escape death on the earth and trusted some researchers' words, claiming that there might be water on Kepler-438b. But what would they do if they fail to find water there? Could they go back to the earth? The answer was "NO WAY," because it was a one-way journey.

Allan also had no idea what would happen to them. Like the spaceship, floating in space, Allan's thoughts had been staying afloat, taking him to different eras and areas. After a short while, he decided not to think about anything. Even the thought of death made his hair stand on end. He looked at Alice. She had been mummied in her spacesuit. What are they going to do with her body after they land? Will they bury her? Is it possible that she is reborn after they set foot on Kepler-438b? Is there any death on Kepler-438b or will they have an eternal life?

He wished Alice was alive, and they could exchange a few words and share their minds. Ache had nested in his back. He had lost track of the time and had no idea how long their journey had already lasted: 10 hours, 10 days, 10 weeks? Stress, death phobia and the em.bodi.ment of death, sitting next to him, had made him sleepless. He had read that man can last about 10 days without sleep, so perhaps he could use it as a measure for his trip duration. But are time units similar here and there? His mind boggled!

Allan
Who hears me?

No one replied! Are they still alive? He felt he had lost lots of weight on the way. His spacesuit was not as tight as it was, and he could move his shoulders more freely in it. He started to move a little bit to descend the ache that was ruling over his body. His buttocks were the most painful area. He felt that they were no longer curved but flat.

His voice sounded soar, so he tried to clear his throat.

Allan
Uhmm . . . does anybody hear me?

Alex
Yes.

Allan
What's going to happen to us?

Alex
That's my question!

Allan
So who knows?

Doctor
Loudspeaker

Allan
Alex, are your family members ok?

Alex
Still alive!

Allan
Great! Good to have your family with you!

Alex
So why didn't you bring yours?

Allan
My wife and I divorced some years ago.

Alex
How about your girlfriend?

Allan
My girlfriend?! I have no girlfriend.

Alex
Really?! Several magazines wrote about your relationship.

Allan
They were all fake news!

Alex
I see! Does your wife know about your journey?

Allan
I don't know. I am dead to her.

Alex
Why?

Allan
I was charged with a sexual assault by my secretary, and right after
the word spread, she left me.

Alex
Yes, I remember it!

Allan
Believe me that it was only a false charge. She wanted to black-mail me, trying to force me to pay her 100,000 dollars, and after I refused, she filed a charge against me. That made my life a hell for a while. I really didn't know how to escape reporters and camera-men who were everywhere even in my bathroom! They made me notorious. They ruined my fame, name and family life even before the charge is proved in the court.

Alex
I see!

Allan cleared his mind and voice:

Allan
Media had made life really hard on the earth. I'm happy that there won't be any reporter and cameraman on Kepler-438b, so we can live without the noise and strife of media.

Alex
Don't be so sure!

Captain
This is the Captain! We are fast approaching Kepler-438b, and we hope that we land soon. After landing, you will stay inside the cabin until the Co-pilot and I survey the area around landing zone. After the survey, we might issue a permit for evacuating the space-ship. If so, depending on the atmosphere condition, we spend some time out to get used to our new home. I'll give you further instruc-tions after landing. The condition on Kepler-438b will determine how we will proceed with our breathing mode. In addition to some water and nutrition supply, we have seven guns of five different types to protect ourselves against unexpected threats. We also have two cameras to record our life conditions and send them to NASA if we manage to hold any connection.

Allan
Allan

Allan
Camera again! It seems that we have been born with cameras and die with cameras!

The spaceship started to shake again. Its sudden vertical and horizontal turbulences made some passengers feel sick and worried.

Alex
What's going on?

Allan
I don't know. Perhaps Kepler is not receptive to us!

Alex
We are a foreign object by the way just like a sperm in a womb.

Allan
Perhaps Kepler has some counteracting forces that prevent us from landing.

Orbit 7

Death & Breath

After a long survey, which seemed longer than the whole journey, the Captain had some new information to share with the passengers. Gravity on Kepler-438b's surface was about 30% lower than it was on the earth. Thus, a person who weighed 100 kg on the earth weighed only 70 kg on Kepler-438b. That meant that life on Kepler-438b was more convenient for those passengers who suffered from obesity on the earth. The Captain tried to explain these proportionalities by the following formula:

$$g = m/r^2$$

where **g** is the surface gravity, expressed as a multiple of the earth's, which is 9.8 m/s²

m is its mass, expressed as a multiple of the earth's mass, equal to 5.9 kg and

r its radius, expressed as a multiple of the earth's radius, which is equal to 6.41 km.

Such technical information seemed to be incomprehensible to almost all passengers, who started to stare at their fellows in bewilderment. What the Captain did not reveal after all to all was that for unknown reasons their oxygen meters had failed to function, and they had no idea how they should measure the oxygen level on Kepler-438b! The Captain and the Co-pilot were stressed out! How could they shoot the trouble, or would the trouble shoot them?! Desperately, the Captain issued an order to leave the spaceship. Upon hearing this, all passengers who were still alive cheered up! However, their cheers contained a sense of an.x.iety. No one knew what was waiting for them!

During that interval, Barron was thinking that the sea, earth and sky are one; yesterday, today and tomorrow are one; morning, noon and night are one; past, present and future are one. How about birth, death and post-obit? How about limbo, hell and heaven? How about black, yellow and white races? How about low, middle and high classes? Are they one, too?

Unlike the earthly flights, wherein the first class passengers leave the aircraft first, here the first class passengers left the spaceship last, and instead, the third class passengers evacuated the spaceship first. This showed that their blood was bluer than Allan's blood. The Captain advised the passengers to leave the dead buddies in the spaceship and evacuate the spaceship one by one carefully after the light above their heads went green. He also wanted them to stay as close as possible to the spaceship to avoid any possible threat.

The lights for Allan and Alice were green. He looked at Alice once again, but in fact, the light of Alice's life was red forever. So as the Captain had said, she had to stay in. Allan stood up, but a great backache made him sit again. How could he walk past Alice? The

36

space was too narrow for him to pass to the isle. There was no one to help, since the fellow passengers next and behind him had already left the spaceship, and the other passengers could not stand up without the Captain's permit. He stood up again and with lots of struggles, he walked past her by. For a second, some parts of their bodies overlapped! Unlike many other passengers, who left the spaceship in groups of two, he was a.l.one. He wished he had someone to ac.company him.

As soon as he reached the exit, he curiously lOOked out. It was extremely dark. He cowered in fear as he descended the very narrow and shaky stairs. He could hear the tumults of the crowd, gathered below the stairs. As soon as he set his foot on the surface of Kepler-438b, he felt that he grew in stature.

Allan
Oh, I feel I am taller now.

Andy Weir
True, that's because of the lower level of gravity.

Allan
Andy, are you still alive? I heard that you passed away some years ago.

Andy Weir
Authors do not die. Have you read my book *The Martian*?

Allan
No! With numerous companies and staff, I had no time to read anything. Every now and then, I just looked at my photos in magazines and newspapers. I didn't find time even to read what they

had written about me. But good to have you here. Where on earth are we? Why is it so dark? Is it always dark?

Andy
We are no longer on the earth! It's dark, cause it's night now.

Allan
I see. Do you think we see the morning, or we will be mourning before that?

Someone
We have come a long way to see the morning, don't we?!

Someone's soft voice caught Allan's attention.

Allan
True! Whom do I have honor to speak with?

Someone
I'm Kim Atwood. the grandchild of Margaret Atwood.

Allan stretched his hand and shook hands with her. Exchanging a few words with a pretty lady soothed him! Her words had relieved and energized him and made the dark light! Her warmth attracted him just like a magnate attracting a nail. By now, he had totally forgotten about Andy.

Kim
Do you have any idea how long our journey lasted?

Allan
No, but the ache reigning in my body shows that we've been on the way for long.

Kim let out a nervous giggle, a giggle that evoked a twisted smile from Allan, but soon she suppressed her giggle.

Kim

We've lost track of time. Time in this journey is senseless. I feel a horrible ache in my neck and back part.

Allan

The good point is that the weather is cool here. By the way, do you have any company in this journey?

Kim

No! I'm a.l.one.

Kim's reply made Allan feel better. What could be better than a company that could complement him in his space life!

Kim

How about you? Do you have any company?

Allan

Yes, I have several companies.

Kim

Really?! Where are they?

Allan

On the earth, but no one buys my companies anymore.

Allan sometimes wants to be funny, but his sense of humor usually makes other people shocked rather than laugh! This sense brought the shrill sound of his laughter to an abrupt stop. Bit by bit, some more passengers got off the spaceship, and the crowd became larger. After a while, the Captain appeared. His appearance made the crowd silent. They were all willing to hear the Captain's words, and each word counted. Words are worlds, but sometimes we waste them just as we waste the world, Kim pondered.

Captain
Welcome to Kepler-438b, our new home. I hope we can build our new life here from the scratch. As you see, it is dark here, so we have to wait to have some light. You can walk around the space-ship slowly but together. Keep the oxygen valves open until further notice. I will walk in front of the crowd, the Co-pilot walks behind the crowd to oversee you and the Doctor walks in the middle. By the way, do you have any question?

Somebody
What do we do after the walk?

Captain
We return to the cabin and stay there until it becomes light. Then, we will start our discovery.

Allan
How long shall we carry this unsuitable suit?

Captain
Until we reach stability.

Alex
What shall we do if life would be impossible without oxygen tanks?

Captain
Ummmm

Captain
Co-pilot

The Captain's hesitation caused a kerfuffle in the crowd. It was a vital question and a question of vitality! Hadn't they thought about this before the journey? This is a matter of life and death after earth.

Captain
Let me answer this question a bit later, but for now, let's keep two thirds of the cylinder valve open and check your breathing status. Allan was hesitant to do so. He wanted to see what happens to those who do it before him. They continued walking, and they had already turned around the spaceship ten times.

Captain
Please stop! How do you feel now?

Allan
Fine!

Captain
Let me check your heart beats.

As soon as the Captain approached Allan, he found that he has not decreased the oxygen valve. This made the Captain furious!

Captain
Why haven't you reduced the valve?! Why didn't you follow the instructions?

Allan
I'm terribly sorry!

The Captain shouted at Allan. With his head down, Allan showed no reaction, and this gave the Captain more self-confidence, looking for any mistake by anyone to show his authority.

Despite his anger, the Captain had a great feeling. These wealthy people had ruled the whole entire world for centuries, and in the battle between knowledge and money, the former had always lost the game. He had spent all his years at schools, universities, academia and research institutes, conducting research; however, no one knew him, and his financial status, compared to these affluent and influential figures, was incomparable. Now he had a great opportunity to command. Now it was knowledge that could beat money for the first time in the history of humanity!

After some more rounds, the Captain commanded his men to enter the cabin. While walking around the spaceship, the passengers moved disorderly, and that messed up their classes, but after entering the cabin, the classes were intact again.

As the Captain instructed them, they will sleep in the cabin until they have daylight. They could not see anything, except some dim rays of light and some bright spots in the sky. Allan's supposition was that they never step on Kepler-438b. How many suppositions we have that are wrong, and we are not aware of them! How many things that our teachers and parents have taught us but wrongly! Allan remembered that once in a street in Detroit a small girl, who looked hungry, asked her mom for Sushi. "Mom, I want *Susi*." "It is not Susi," her mom retorted, "it's *Shusi*. Now repeat after me: Shusi!" and the little girl mispronounced it as her mom did!

Allan sat on his own seat. He wished that Kim was sitting next to him. What will happen if someone else wins Kim's heart? A prompt action was required. After a while, he closed his eyes and soon fell asleep. In his dream, he saw that he suddenly lost all his hairs and went bald! Then, he saw Alice pleading him to marry her.

Allan
But I'm bald!

Alice
No problem! Bald men are sexier!

Allan
Are you crazy?

Alice
No, scientists have found that bald men are bold.

Allan
But . . .

Alice
But me no buts!

Then, Alice started kissing Allan passionately, and the lovely scene made the passengers erupt in cheers! However, Allan no longer loved Alice and was reluctant to kiss Alice. What could he do? Shall he go toward Kim and proposes her? What if she declines his proposal?

How spacious is my heart

It loves all, that's its art

It carries them in its cart

One by one, at a time

My heart has many p|a|r|t|s

Wherein drawn many charts

One comes in, one de|parts

I climb, I climb, is that crime?

Like other passengers, the Captain was grinning from ear to ear. Then, he began speaking:

Captain
Very good morning! This is the Captain speaking. Fortunately, we see some light now; however, we need to wait for some more light. We have a hard day today, and thus, we need to prepare well. You can have your nutrition capsules now. To avoid any possible threats, the Co-pilot and I will have a survey of the outside condition before we leave the spaceship.

The words of the Captain woke Allan up! He gazed at Alice's face from under her helmet visor. She was smiling. Was she happy with her life after death? Allan remembered how he was irritated even with the thoughts of death and how much he was afraid of a dead body, but this journey had reset his mind set. Death was no longer frightening to him! He had had a dead body as his buddy during a long trip wherein death was chasing him. What was the interpretation of a dream wherein a dead body kisses you? He thought. Was he going to die soon? He looked at Alice again.

Allan
How do you feel Alice?

Alice
I'm fine! How about you?

Allan could not believe his ears. He rubbed his eyes.

Allan
Are you alive?

Allan
Allan

Alice

Yes, I was thinking that all angels, save the Angel of Death, are unemployed. For instance, Gabriel was super busy while God used to send prophets over and over again to direct man to the right path, and he was always on mission between heaven and earth, transferring the divine messages to the prophets. However, since God has stopped sending any more prophets, Gabriel has lost his job or has been retired. On the contrary, the Angel of Death has always been working nonstop since the beginning of history, and he has been neither tired nor retired.

Allan
Allan
Allan

Allan was shocked. He started shouting, "She is alive! She is alive!" Soon the Doctor appeared and examined Alice.

Allan
Doctor
Alice

Doctor

No zignz of life detected! Zez dead.

After a while, the Captain ordered the passengers to leave the spaceship according to his instructions. Andy eagerly looked out of the exit door. He was curious to see how Kepler-438b looked like, and whether it had any similarity with what he had read or watched about the space and other planets? He could detect a great difference between what he had in mind and what he could see with his own eyes. Seeing is believing! He did not believe his eyes! It seemed that he had been deceived by some fictions and movies that had simulated other planets based on their own surmises. Everything looked extremely different.

Andy
Andy
Andy

He had fixed his eyes on vast Kepler-438b while descending the stairs. The rocky land was a combination of black, brown, chestnut, white and grey. It looked like a mosaic, a granite. Is the whole Kepler just like that? If so, their chances were dim to find any signs of life. However, like the earth, Kepler-438b should have different climates, Andy thought. They had to explore and see. Perhaps there were other spots with water. How about oxygen? They were still carrying and using oxygen cylinders, and no one knew what would happen if they run out of oxygen, water and nutrition capsules? Some passengers had left the spaceship at the behest of the Captain, while some others from the second and first classes were still in.

Soon all passengers set foot on Kepler-438b. The Captain gave some instructions and urged everyone to obey him. Then, he ordered Allan and Alex to remove dead bodies from the spaceship. Allan did not favour the Captain's order, but he did not dare to disobey. Reluctantly, he assisted Alex to remove two bodies with difficulties. The narrow isle and staircase had made their job more demanding. Sweats rolled down their foreheads and entered their eyes. After the Captain observed their tiredness, he appointed two other men from the third class passengers to continue the job. They also removed two bodies, both kids! Their parents' wailings made some passengers sob. Three more bodies were removed from the spaceship. Seven buddies had lost their lives on the way. The Captain then gave a spade to Andy and Somebody.

Captain
Move the buddies over there, remove their spacesuits and bury them. The Doctor will ob.serve you.

Just like other passengers, Allan looked sad. Why did this happen to us? While murmuring this question, something inside him retorted, "Because of your deeds!"

The Captain, the Co-pilot, Doctor and Philip Windsor held four different but strange guns. The Captain had the biggest one, which gave him a sense of pride and privilege. Allan wished to have one of those guns to both protect himself and get some credits for it and walk ahead of the crowd.

As soon as the burial job was over, the Captain ordered the passengers to stay in three lines. Allan and some other passengers struggled to stay in front of the line. He pushed back some passengers just to be in front. Being a forerunner always gave him a great feeling. As soon as the passengers formed the lines, the Captain appointed the Co-pilot, Doctor and Philip in front of each line, and he stood in front of the whole crowd, cleared his throat and made a speech.

Captain
Great! First, a minute's silence for all those who lost their lives on the way.

Allan

One minute?! Do we have the same units of time here as we used on the earth? Does anybody have a watch here?

The Captain frowned at him.

<table>
<tr><td></td><td>**Captain**</td><td></td></tr>
<tr><td>**Doctor**</td><td>**Co-pilot**</td><td>**Philip**</td></tr>
<tr><td>**Allan**</td><td>**Alex**</td><td>**Andy**</td></tr>
<tr><td>. . .</td><td>. . .</td><td>. . .</td></tr>
</table>

Captain

Now, since the gravity level here is a bit lower than the earth's gravity level, I think we can remove our spacesuits. I hope that we do not have serious issues. But to be on the safe side, we start with the people in the second front row. They remove their spacesuits, and if they had no problems, we proceed with others.

He then pointed to Allan, Alex and Andy and asked them to remove their spacesuits. This increased Allan's h.e.a.r.t.b.e.a.t.s and stress level. The Captain also asked the Doctor, Co-Pilot and Philip to give their hands to Allan, Alex and Andy to remove their uncomfortable and heavy spacesuits.

Allan had a very bad feeling, cursing himself for his struggle to stand in front. That was to hug death earlier than others. He was so frightened that he wanted to defy the Captain's order, but after remembering the Captain's last night violent reaction, he surrendered. He was still he.sit.ant to remove his spacesuit and attempted to do it as s.low as possible. Life was getting more mysterious, and he didn't want to die after all! He felt like a lab rat, fallen in the hands of a crazy "scientist."

48

Finally, Allan, Alex and Andy removed their unsuitable suits. Sometimes we just resist against discarding some habits, traditions, customs, costumes and beliefs that are just like burdens to us, thinking that life would be impossible without them, but as soon as we dump them, we feel better.

The Captain observed Allan, Alex and Andy for a while, and after he got sure that they have a "nor.mal" life, he ordered the other passengers to remove their spacesuits. However, the Captain and his three assistants did not change their own suits until everyone did. The Captain wanted to see the health conditions of all before taking any action. Owing to the lack of gravity, the passengers felt to be straighter with less attachment to the surface of Kepler-438b.

They all had a better feeling despite the ache they all had all over their bodies. The Captain asked them to freely move their hands and stretch their bodies. Right after that, he asked them to reduce the valves of their oxygen cylinders to see how it will go with less oxygen. Then, they decided to walk together and explore the areas around the spaceship so that they would return to it for their night stay.

The marching crowd looked curiously at different and distant locations, and sometimes they bent down to touch the granite-looking rocks that were not promising to host any water in them. How long could they survive in this barren land? Are any people, animals or aliens living here? Before long, a passenger who looked worn out suddenly stopped and sat down. One of the passengers kept the Captain posted, and he ordered the crowd to stop.

Captain
What's wrong?

Emma McCain
I'm dead tired! How far shall we go? What are we looking for in this barren land? There is no water here! No oxygen! Nothing! What happens if . . .

Captain
Enough is enough.

Emma's words came as a complete surprise to passengers who looked both anxious and happy that finally one person dared to voice their concerns. After a while, the Captain, who had been dazed by some of the passengers' reactions, looked around nervously, cleared his throat and spoke in low tones:

Captain
Mmm in fact, we have to explore this planet as much as we can to find signs of life. Kepler-438b is as big as the earth, and we are hopeful to find water before it gets late. As for oxygen, we have been doing well with half oxygen amount, but I have no idea by now whether we can survive without oxygen cylinders. Let's see! These words made the whole crowd drone on.

Barron
If so, why we were told during the trainings that the conditions of Kepler-438b are just as the earth's?!

Kim
If there is no oxygen, how would we survive?! Why were we sent to here? To prepone our death!

The crowd's continuous humming sound irritated the Captain, who looked helpless. Allan could see the drops of sweat on the Captain's forehead. He had never seen the Captain so vulnerable. After a short while, the Captain cleared his throat again and continued:

Captain
No worries! Calm down, folks! Be patient and trust me! Now let us try to close the oxygen valve and see how we can go on with no oxygen.

These words made the situation even worse. The crowd's buzz turned to sound and fury. A couple of passengers started to shout angrily and blamed the Captain for their premature deaths. The Captain attempted to regain his power and raised his voice:

Captain
Shut up, idiots, or else . . . .

He did not complete his sentence, but that was enough to spread a net of silence on the whole coward crowd. The passengers had no other choice. Their life and death were in the hands of the Captain. The Captain, who looked penitent, continued his speech:

Captain
Allan! Close the oxygen valve in full and remove your oxygen mask right now. The Doctor will control your condition. If everything goes on well, then, we will try this on all.

Allan's heart was in his mouth! He lOOked around desperately, asking himself, "why me?!" He wished to refuse the Captain's dictate, but after reviewing how the Captain mistreated him the night before, he decided to go for it. The whole crowd has fixed their gazes on Allan's head. They were waiting to see his suffering and suffocation. The Doctor was standing next to him to control his conditions, but Allan did not trust the Doctor. If he was a good doctor, seven passengers had not died on the way! He used to be an atheist while living in prosperity on the earth; however, this journey had made him a believer. There had happened some moments wherein he helplessly resorted to God for help and even murmured some prayers and religious songs, which he had learned during his school years. Involuntarily, Allan closed the oxygen valve in full and removed his mask.

Kim
Doctor
Captain
Alex
Andy
Philip
Emma
Barron
Alice
Somebody
Wilhelm
Co-pilot

Allan felt dizzy. He had a horrible headache, and all of a sudden, he fell down. This made all his fellow passengers give a yell of fear. The Doctor sat cross-legged on the ground to examine his vital signs.

Doctor
Doctor
Doctor

Doctor
Breazing, blood prezure, body temperazure and pulze are . . . .
. . . nor.mal. All hiz four primary vital zignz are working well. I
zink he haz fainted becauz of trauma.

Captain
Are you sure? Don't you need to attach his oxygen mask again?

The Doctor stood up and whispered something in the Captain's
ear. This made all passengers more stressed. What was he hiding
from them? Did he tell lies about Allan's conditions? Did he notify
the Captain of Allan's death? Did he say that he had no hope, and
any further efforts to remove the oxygen cylinders would fail? All
passengers had been also shocked that why the Doctor does not
reattach Allan's oxygen mask? Did he want to survey how they all
would die one after the other? No one was aware of the Doctor's
plan, save the Captain.

Orbit 6
Suffocation & Resurrection

Allan
Where . . . am . . . I?

Doctor
Here wiz uz! How do you feel?

Allan
Allan
Allan

Doctor
Let me zek your eyez. Philip, would you help him zit up?

Philip
Sure!

Everybody was delighted to see that Allan is alive and can live on without any oxygen mask. The Doctor proceeded with his examinations and reported that Alan had become too feeble and required further nutrition. The Doctor then asked him whether he had any breathing problems, or if he could detect any air quality difference between the earth and Kepler-438b?

Everyone was waiting for Allan to respond.

Allan
Allan
Allan

Allen still had some headache and was unable to speak. The Doctor repeated his questions one by one and word by word, making hand gestures while talking to get sure that Allan had fully understood him. After a while, Allan started to speak. His words, formed with care through the slur in his voice, had made it hard for the Doctor to comprehend him. Every word counted, and thus, the Captain also sat down next to the Doctor and Philip to hear what Allan tried to utter. This made other passengers more curious, encouraging them to come closer and gather around Allan, the Doctor, Philip and the Captain.

Allan's slurred words showed that there were some differences between the air quality on Kepler-438b and on the earth. Based on Allan's words, the air seemed to be thicker on the former, and thus, he suffered from a sore throat, making it hard for him to breathe normally. The Doctor asked some questions about whether Allan had any irritation in his eyes and ears, too, and Allan nodded. His response made those observing the scene and hearing his words upset, leaving them with a big question that how long they could live in such an unidentified atmosphere of agony? One could clearly read sorrow in their faces.

Wilhelm Miller, who used to produce chemical weapons for generations, started pondering what their products, including chlorine gas, phosgene, mustard gas, tabun and sarin gas, have done to mankind throughout the history! How they had made a good life for themselves at the cost of horrible deaths of *others*. He and his family had been sentenced to a painful and traumatic suffocation with inert gas asphyxiation. As a form of asphyxiation, which happens in the absence or low level of oxygen, inert gas asphyxiation contains no toxic and does not attack heart or hemoglobin. Rather, it lowers the oxygen concentration in blood cells and eventually k.ills man! He remembered how the same method was used to slaughter livestock and birds.

Wilhelm Miller
What I did, now has returned to me like a boomerang.

Captain
What?

Wilhelm
Nothing!

While following Allan's hard times, other passengers, just like Wilhelm, were thinking about their own deeds on the earth. Is this a revenge? Does the hand of destiny has dragged them to such a lethal atmosphere to give it back to them?

For every action, there is an equal but opposite reaction, Wilhelm thought!

Doctor
Az I zee, hiz eyez irritazon iz getting better. How iz your zroat, Allan?

Allan
¡suɹɹnq · · · ʇI

The Doctor gave him some water.

Doctor
How do you feel now?

Allan
Allan
Allan

All passengers had horrible feelings. Allan was a mirror reflecting their own tragic end; an end no one would learn about! With sobs of despair, some of them sat down, covering their faces with their hands. The Captain, who now had become totally impotent and dependent upon the Doctor, shouted:

Captain
Why doesn't he reply?! Is he dead?

The Doctor quickly examined Allan's vital signs.

Doctor
Doctor
Doctor

Doctor
He'z in a coma and needz to be attazed to life zupport mazines.

Captain
Life support machines?! Where can we bring life support machines?!

After a pause, he asked:

Captain
Does he die if he is not attached to life support machines?!

Doctor
I don't k.no.w! Probably yes!

The response made the Captain stand up. The death of Allan could be the death of all or rather a countdown for their deaths.

Captain
Please do whatever you can to save him.

The Doctor who seemed to be careless to what the Captain said continued his job.

Doctor
Do you hear me?

Allan
Allan
Allan

Doctor
It'z baffling! Hiz pupilz are equal, round and reactive to light and accommodazon. A pupil iz abnormal if it failz to dilate in dim lighting or doz not rezpond to light or accommodazon.

It was as if the Doctor was preparing for a medical exam. He was just repeating what he had studied in medical books and papers during his internship.

Doctor
Rezpiratory rate: 10 per minute
Pulz: 50 per minute; bradycardia
Temperature: normal
So whatz wrong? What'z zent him into a coma? Why doz he faint?

The Doctor had become powerless. It was as if knowledge just like wealth was no longer a privilege on Kepler-438b. It was rather a burden, since everyone expected the Doctor to do something!

No one was hopeful and helpful. To other passengers, Allan was dead, and they were in line. The mental pres.sure was so high that another passenger also fainted. The Doctor, the Captain and the Co-pilot had become clumsy. They lost their control and had no idea how to handle the problem. The Doctor left Allan and rushed toward the newly fainted passenger.

Doctor
Move pazengerz to another locazon.

Captain
Alright!

The Captain asked the passengers to follow him. They walked about 10 meters away. The Captain wanted them to turn their back to where the Doctor was, and he stayed right in front of the crowd to see what was happening over there.

Allan
Alice, how do you feel?

Alice
I'm OK! How about you?

Allan
I'm suffocating!

Alice
Don't fret! You'll be fine soon. I had hard times before suffocating, but now I feel good. See you soon!

All of a sudden, Allan sat up! His death could not be that shocking that his life was! How is it possible?! He had been resurrected.

The Captain could not believe his eyes! He left his words incomplete, hurriedly ran toward Allan, sat down, stretched his hands and hugged him. Allan stood erect.

Captain
Allan, I'm happy that you are alive. How do you feel?

Allan
I'm, I'm . . . . .

Captain
You're what?! Any pain or irritation?

Allan
Allan
Allan

Doctor
How iz your zroat?

Allan
The . . . air is . . . . polluted.

The Captain grinned from ear to ear. He jumped up and down. How could it be possible? Sometimes miracles happen exactly when we lose all our hope! All passengers looked cheerful and hopeful. It was as if they had been reborn! Allan's survival was their survival.

The Doctor helped the other passenger recover, too. So far so good; however, they had a long way to go.

Captain
Now, it is time for all of us to remove our oxygen masks.

The Captain's statement was enough to dry out the roots of joy that had just germinated in the hearts of all passengers and to shoot the shoots of the seeds that had just emerged from the soil of their minds.

Captain
We will remove the masks in groups of two, so that we would be able to take a good care of you.

No one wanted to be the first to do so. Having seen the tough conditions and sufferings of Allan, who had a narrow escape, the other passengers did not want to risk their lives. All were hesitant. Will we lose our life or will we survive? They had no idea!

Captain
Let's continue with Alex and Andy.

Andy
What? No, not me!

Alex
Me? Are you kidding?

They both took some steps back. This created a challenge to the Captain, who always wished to be obeyed without any objection. What could he do? Would he shout and force them to remove their masks? But it might cause a trauma!

The Captain looked around helplessly, thought for a while, shook his head and cleared his voice:

Captain
Let's continue our exploration!

His new statement rest.ored peace to the agitated crowd who looked like defenceless chickens in the hands of a slaughterer.The Captain asked them to walk in three rows as before. Allan was still suffering from a headache; however, he was the only one who had no mask. The Captain was curious to learn more about Allan's condition, so he called Allan to the forefront and walked with him shoulder to shoulder. He complained about the tainted air, which had caused him a horrible headache and irritation. He had managed to walk shoulder to shoulder with the Captain and even in front of the Doctor, the Co-pilot and Philip, who had guns. The Captain was dependent upon him, since he was the only one who could encourage other passengers to remove their masks.

Captain
I envy you Allan. Now that you have got rid of your nasty mask, perhaps you can talk to your other fellow passengers to do what you have done. What do you think?

Allan was fully aware of the great winning card he had in hand, but he knew that he would lose his credit right after other passengers remove their masks. How could he benefit from this privilege before it got late, he pondered.

Captain
What do you think?

Allan
Didn't you hear my thoughts?

Captain
What thoughts?!

Allan
Mmm . . . nothing! I think it's too early to ask them remove their masks. We have enough oxygen cylinders, don't we?

Captain
Yes!

Allan
So let's do it tomorrow.

Captain
Alright!

As a result of his big risk, Allan had managed to attain a great position; however, he had forgotten about Kim. What mattered the most for him at that stage was to elevate his rank. If so, many Kims could be his.

In the evening, the Captain first commanded the crowd to take a nutrition capsule and then return to the spaceship. It was safer to sleep in the spaceship than in the open air. During the first-day exploration, they had not found any trace of water and life, but they were fully contented with what Allan had achieved.

Orbit 5
Life after Earth

Early in the morning, the Captain got up and awakened the passengers. The passengers had trouble getting up. That was the first night that they had slept without their spacesuits. They had to start their explorations as soon as they could.

The Captain approached Allan and urged him to make a speech for the whole crowd, describe his good feelings and entice them to remove their oxygen masks.

Allan
Captain! I . . . . would do . . . so, but . . .

Captain
But what?

Allan
But . . . I need . . . .

Captain
What do you need?

Allan
A gun and a group.

Captain
A gun and a group!? But do you know how to even use a professional gun?!

Allan

I know! Granting a gun and a group to me sends a clear message to all that if they obey your orders, they would elevate their status, and vice versa.

Captain	Allan
Captain	Allan
Captain	Allan
Captain	Allan

The Captain liked the idea and immediately asked the Co-pilot to give a gun to Allan. He then promised to appoint Allan as a group leader if he could accomplish his mission. Allan was on cloud nine. He surv.eyed his gun with a great plea.sure for a while. It was totally different from his hunting guns, and he had no idea how to use it.

Happily, he addressed the passengers:

Allan

Good morning everyone! As you know, I removed my oxygen mask yesterday. I faced some issues at first, but now as you see, I have a good feeling and can live without oxygen cylinder. I just talked to the Captain, and he told me that unfortunately our oxygen will be over soon. So I recommend you to get rid of these nasty cylinders right now.

Allan

Captain	Co-pilot	Philip
Doctor	Alex	Andy
. . .	. . .	. . .

Allan

Don't worry! It doesn't hurt. It takes a few seconds, and then, you'll be fine. Trust me.

Allan

Captain	**Co-pilot**	**Philip**
Doctor	**Alex**	**Andy**
. . .	. . .	. . .

Andy
Sorry, I don't believe you. I saw how you swooned.

Emma
Yes, he's right! I remember how you collapsed, foaming at the mouth.

Allan
True, true, but . . .

Kim
But what?

Kim's words did catch Allan's eyes. Allan remembered his affection to Kim, which had been soon suffocated as a result of his desire for gun and group!

Allan
You know . . . I . . . mean . . .

He tried to regain his self-confidence and went on . . .

Allan
Oxygen will be over soon. What can you do without it? Do or Die! That's the question. You can get rid of this mask now just like a butterfly breaking out of a cocoon or die within it. It's up to you, and I have no other words. Thank you!

Allan failed. He was hopelessly walking toward his own position while touching his gun and looking at his group. He felt sad, but what else could he do?! Could he remove the passengers' masks by force?! Nothing came to his mind. He felt like a loser. He had to return his gun to the Captain. How sad it was for Allan to lose what he had gained with some difficulty, but it was not sadder than losing all his power, possessions and properties on the earth, he reflected with sadness.

Suddenly, a voice interrupted his reflections.

Wilhelm
So do you guarantee that I won't lose my life if I remove my mask?

This question revived hope in Allan. He stopped where he was and looked at the Captain with a smile of satisfaction.

Allan

Captain	**Co-pilot**	**Philip**
Doctor	**Alex**	**Andy**
. . .	. . .	. . .

Allan
Yes! Don't fret! Just go for it. I'm sure that . . .

He was so excited that he couldn't end his sentence. But what would happen if Wilhelm loses his life? Allan contemplated. Nothing! He could be just like the Captain who had already killed several people. One did not make a big difference in this equation according to Allan's mind.

He had a feeling that *he* was the Captain. He had been asked for his mind, and just like the Captain, he saw himself in a position to talk about a vital issue related to life and death of passengers. He didn't expect it. How fast everything might change!

Allan
I believe we must help each other. Together we are stronger, aren't we?

Allan returned to his former position and stood in front of the crowd.

Allan

Captain	Co-pilot	Philip
Doctor	Alex	Andy
. . .	. . .	. . .

Allan
One way is to share our experience. For instance, I had an experience, which you think of as dreadful, while for me it was sweet. To me, you are brave, and only brave people like us can do such grave works. So remove your mask. Let other passengers see how easy it is. I'm sure they all will race over to do it right after you. They will owe you and I for good as their saviors.

Allan stole a furtive glance at the Captain, who looked cross. It seemed that he was not happy with Allan's last claims, implicitly introducing himself as their brave savior!

Allan
What do you think, Wilhelm?

He was not sure if Wilhelm accepts his mortal proposal.

Wilhelm
OK. I go for it.

Allan
Really?! Andy, help Wilhelm to remove his oxygen mask. Doctor, observe the process.

Allan felt like a hero. He was commanding others what to do. He b.linked at the Captain. Perhaps he wanted to remind the Captain of his promise.

Soon Wilhelm lied down and the Doctor carefully removed his oxygen mask. Since he had the experience of inhaling some other gases such as helium, neon, carbon dioxide, etc. in his lab and factory, testing and producing chemical weapons, unlike Allan, he faced no serious issue, and after a short while, he stood up. Despite some dizziness, he pretended to be fine and strong. This motivated some other passengers to remove their masks; however, it was not as easy as it went for Wilhelm. Three passengers faced severe health problems, and three passengers, due to age, breathing problems and stress, lost their lives.

Ten passengers out of one hundred had already lost their lives. The death of three more created a tension for all, except for Allan who enjoyed walking with a gun in the crowd and talked to them like a commander-in-chief. The Captain ordered a couple of passengers to carry and bury the dead bodies where seven other bodies had been buried. Everybody had headache and sore throat as well as eye and ear irritations. The Doctor had no idea how he could help the passengers to get rid of the headache and irritation. The Captain and the Doctor blamed the high levels of radiation on Kepler-438b as the main reason for their respiration problems; however, they were unable to offer any solutions. It seemed that the passengers had to live with these health issues until the end of their lives.

The next day, the Captain arranged the crowd in four lines and appointed the fourth group under the protection of Allan. Despite his horrible headache, the Captain spent some time surveying some other directions with his binoculars.

Captain
Doctor, this planet is a maze! I've spent all my life studying and researching on space, but what I see and what I expected to see are as different as day and night!

Doctor
You're right! I've alzo zpent all my life ztudying medical zienz and human anatomy, but phyzical condizon of people here bafflez me!

The Captain ordered the passengers to take some tools and all their nutrition capsules and water bottles from the spaceship and follow him toward his desired direction. Every now and then, he looked back at the spaceship, wondering whether they see this place again. Will they get lost and lose their lives on the way? He could not anticipate what would happen to them. Perhaps they find water, who knows!

Hope is always the last reserve

But a strong one

Making us persist and pursue

Despite seemingly impossible impasses

The Captain asked the crowd to chant a song together to feel stronger and forget about their pains and losses, but not all passengers chanted. How could a parent who has just lost his *Beloved* chant?!

On the way, Allan was thinking what the difference between him and the Captain was! Why his gun was smaller and why he did not have binoculars? He believed that if he had the equipment that the Captain had, he could be a better leader. He remembered how he encouraged others to remove their masks after the Captain failed!

The crowd had become totally hopeless. Every now and then, the Captain ordered the exhausted crowd to stop and take some rest, and he took the opportunity to look around with his binoculars. Everywhere had covered with a black, brown, grey, white dry soil, which signified death! Like others, the Captain believed that their chance to find water was dim. Despite this, they had to struggle.

Orbit 4

Trail of Tears

A few days went by. The days seemed several times longer than on the earth, while its nights seemed shorter than the earthly nights. They stopped as soon as it got dark and slept while those who had guns took turns to stay awake and watch others. However, even before many passengers fall asleep, it was light, and they had to get up and continue their exploration. By now, two more passengers, Andy and Alex, had guns, walking behind the lines. This issue had saddened Allan, who believed that he had done a great job and deserved to get a gun while Andy and Alex had got guns without any devotion.

Philip
Oh my God! What's that? Wake up! Captain, wake up!

The Captain did not move, so Philip grabbed him by his shoulder and shook him.

Captain
What's wrong?

Philip
Look at there!

Captain
What?! EVERYBODY WAKE UP!

The Captain shouted as loud as he could. Everybody suddenly woke up as if it was the resurrection time! The Captain ordered the crowd to stay in their own groups, commanding all who had guns to stay shoulder to shoulder in front of the crowd and get ready to shoot if necessary.

That was the most horrific moment since they had landed on Kepler-438b. The passengers were trembling, praying or crying.

Emma
What are they?

Kim
I don't know!

Andy
They are aliens. Yes, they are aliens! I've read about them.

Captain
Everybody, lie down on the ground. Only those who have guns stand on their knees and fire as soon as I say. OK?

DoctorCo-pilotPhilipAllanAndyAlex
Yes, Sir!

Everyone was on the ground. In front of the crowd, seven people had sat up with their guns pointed toward a direction wherefrom some unidentified objects were approaching them. In addition to irritation, fear had clutched at their throats. The loud noises of their moves had worsened the situation.

Captain
Ready!

They were all ready to fire. One more word from the Captain sufficed to start a bloody war. Allan looked around. He could see how at the time of danger, all ranks and classifications fade away. Survival was the only thing everyone was thinking of at the time. The unidentified objects were getting closer and closer, and everyone was waiting for the Captain to open fire, but he didn't. What has happened to the Captain? Why didoesn't issue an order?! Did he have a silent heart attack? Is he sound?

It was getting late. The aliens were getting too close.

Doctor
Captain, Captain! Do you hear me? What zall we do?

Captain
Captain
Captain
Captain
Captain

Doctor
Captain, are you ok?

Captain
Shhhhhh, let them get closer.

Allan
But they are too close now.

Allan decided to open fire. That was another critical moment that he could prove himself and stand above the Captain. He was confident that his people would appreciate him after witnessing his bravery. He was determined to take an action, so he suddenly stood up, but to their great surprise, the unidentified objects suddenly changed their route.

Allan
Hehhhhhh

No one knew what happened. Were they dreaming? Did this happen in reality? If yes, who were they? Why they changed their way? Were they scared? Why they were wandering in dark? Did their presence signify life?

Kim
Were they other human beings, sent to Kepler-438b from another country before us?

No one had any idea, but they were relieved that they had left with no clash.

This sense of relief, however, did not last long. Soon the passengers heard some noises from the rear, and when they looked back for the source of weird noises, they found that the same objects were approaching them again. This unanticipated change of route disarranged the array of both the crowd and the gunmen. The Captain, who had also lost his control, commanded the gunmen to turn back and shoot at the unidentified objects.

In a few seconds, the objects were all on the ground. Did they die? Didn't they have anything to protect themselves? What were they made of? What were they? The gunmen were gasping, while the passengers did not dare to stand up! No one dared to approach the unidentified inanimate objects, and the darkness had worsened the situation.

Captain
Let's move on! It's not safe to stay here any longer.

Immediately, the crowd stood up and darted across the dead dark depressing desert. They had no idea where they were heading for. They just wanted to escape the deadly scene and its distresses.

The passengers were heavy-eyed and even dawn glow, creeping into their eyes, failed to make them light-footed. Some of them fell asleep, while many others were full of stress. The Captain authorized the passengers to sleep until further notice and called the gunmen for a private meeting.

The seven gunmen reviewed all their observations. The unidentified objects were still unidentified to them: what were they? They shared their observations, but it didn't help. The Captain believed that the gunmen should also take some rest; otherwise, they won't be able to protect others. The Captain then appointed Allan to watch them and asked all others to sleep. As soon as they fell asleep, Allan got the binoculars. It took him a while to learn how to use such a professional device. Then, he looked around through the binoculars.

Allan
Oh my gosh! Captain! Oh my Captain!

Allan's shout made the Captain jump up!

Captain
What?

Allan
Look at there!

Captain
Aliens again?!

Allan
Watch yourself!

The Captain grabbed the binoculars, rubbed his tired eyes and looked at the direction that Allan pointed. To his great surprise, he perceived that the soil was no longer granite-like but yellow. The yellow stripe of dawn nudging back the darkness had made some changes in the color of the soil.

Captain
Does this change of color signify the existence of life?

The captain lOOked around more carefully with his binoculars.

Captain
What?!

His one-word question was more than enough to bring another worn-out gunman back to consciousness.

Philip
What's wrong?

Captain
Come and see!

Philip stood up quickly and grabbed the binoculars. All other people were curious to know what had aroused the Captain's curiosity.

Philip
Oh my goodness! There are some hills over there. Hills Like White Elephants!

Captain
Hills?! No, I don't think they are hills.

Philip
So what are they?

Allan
Let me see, let me see!

Philip
Captain
Allan

Philip
What's that?

Allan
Some . . .

Captain
Some what?

Allan had no idea what they were; however, he didn't like to look feeble.

Allan
Some . . . land bumps.

Captain
Let's go there. It would be great if Alex stays right here to watch the passengers, and we go there.

The Captain awakened the other gunmen and asked the Co-pilot, the Doctor, Andy, Philip and Allan to accompany him. They moved toward those hills or unknown bumps. On the way, they were all worried about what was waiting for them, except Allan, who was cross! Why the Captain called his name last, while at the time of guarding, he called his name first, he thought!

Before long, the Captain asked his companions to lie on the ground and crawl toward their destination. This had put a great pressure on Allan and others who were not used to such heavy moves. Every now and then, the Captain asked them to stop, and he looked at that point with his binoculars, but he still had trouble detecting what they were. As they got closer, the Captain could observe some very small cabins made of clay. Some were like honeybee pit houses, while some others looked like pueblos. The Captain looked more carefully. Behind them, there were some cliff-sited dwellings. It seemed that some parts of the honeybee pit houses were under the ground, and only a small part of them stood out.

Captain
They are not hills but cabins.

Andy
Cabins?! Whose cabins?!

Allan
Does it mean that some people live here?!

Philip
People?! Impossible! *We* are the only people. *Others* are all aliens!

Andy
Man or alien, that's the question!

Allan
So *what* are they?

Captain
Allan
Co-Pilot
Philip
Doctor

The Captain rubbed his chin.

Captain
Let's see!

They were all scared to approach the bumpy cabins. What if aliens attack them!? They approached the cabins with trembling legs but pretended that they were fearless! On the way, Philip was thinking whether they needed to approach that location at all? What if they would ignore it and avoid any fatal clash? Kepler-438b was vast enough, and they could explore some other parts of it without any problem. His heart suddenly sank. He could not move on.

Captain
What's wrong, Philip? Shake a leg.

Philip
I can't!

Captain
What do you mean? Come on, come on!

Philip
Why don't we forget about this place and explore other places?

Everyone was happy with Philip's courage! It was as if Philip had voiced everyone's concern.

Captain
I understand, but . . .

Philip
But what?!

Captain
This is a good sign of life. The habitants know how to survive, how to find water, how to eat, how to live, and this is exactly what we need to know.

Philip
You are right, but what if we lose our lives! We don't have any common language to communicate with them!

Andy
Are these the dwellings of those whom we killed last night?

The Captain had no answer. He reflected for a while, but then, he moved on. The closer they got to the strange location, the faster their hearts beat. Philip could hear his heart beats in his ear out of f.ear. They were ready to open fire at anybody and anything. Suddenly, the Captain stopped.

Captain
I believe that the moisture content, mineral composition and organic contents are responsible for the soil color change. So there is life here.

Everybody nodded with sinking hearts, except Allan, who was angry with the Captain as the one who always commenced and concluded.

Allan
Why not me?! What's the difference between him and me?!

As soon as they arrived | alived there, the Captain shouted with a trrremmmbllliiing voice:

Captain
Anyone here?

Andy
Allan
Philip
Co-pilot

Captain
Do you h.ear me?

There was no reply. Silence had increased their stress.

Allan
Do they speak English?

Allan's sneer made the Captain groan.

Suddenly, they all heard a strange sound, which threatened them all to death.

Captain
Alarums and excursions!

With no control, they opened fire to where the sound came from. Soon some creatures in different sizes left their dwellings, running from side to side. They looked weird and disgusting. Allan was still shooting aimlessly at them, and with every gunshot, one of those animate beings became inanimate.

The gunmen were still in a shocking mode. They had turned into murderers! They sta.red at each other in disbelief.

Philip
How could we kill several defenceless native creatures?! Last night, we killed some others.

Andy
We only defended ourselves. What matters the most is our own survival.

Captain
Are they defenceless?

Philip
I don't know!

Andy
What I know is that aliens should go to hell. Kill or get killed!

Captain
Doctor
Co-pilot
Allan
Philip

The Captain ordered his companions to be alert. A mistake sufficed to end their lives after all. They looked carefully at the body builds of the dead aliens from far away. They were curious to know what they were made of, what they ate, what they d.rank and how they lived. Silence reigned so much that the gunmen could clearly hear the sound of their companies' breath.

Andy
How long are we going to wait here?

Philip
I don't know! Captain, do you have any idea?

Captain
Doctor, study their anatomy, and we watch you from here.

Doctor
What?! Me?! Oh no pleaz!

Captain
Yes, you are a specialist in anatomy. Go ahead.

Doctor
I'm afraid I can't!

Captain
We accompany you.

Doctor
O . . . K!

The Captain's proposal struck fear into the hearts of all. They moved toward the dead aliens. The Captain, who was disgusted by the sight, ordered Allan and the Doctor to examine the dead bodies, and asked Philip, Andy and the Co-pilot to investigate the aliens' dwellings. Upon approaching the dead aliens, Allan got sick, and the Captain, who had grown a frown and furrow on his face, furiously asked Philip to replace him.

The aliens' body builds and thick brownish skin textures looked like indigenous Americans. Their faces were ancient. However, they had a yellowish thick, sticky and gelatine liquid in their veins in lieu of blood. The Doctor believed that their hypercoagulability resulted from the dry climate. They were hairless and didn't have even a single hair on their bodies.

The Captain looked back over his shoulder and beckoned the Co-pilot to enter one of the aliens' dwellings. Fear had nested in his soul, but he could not disregard the Captain's order. The Co-pilot, who looked he…sit…ant, stepped in the first ca.bin ti.mid.ly. Before entering, he made some noises and banged the short walls of the cabin with the butt of his gun. Every now and then, he expected an unexpected attack from an alien that was in hide. The deeper he explored, the cooler it became. Step by step, he descended the steep walls of the cabin and followed them to a tiny flat room. His small torch could only lighten a couple of meters ahead.

The Co-Pilot found a collection of hand-made portable pot.tery and moved them out with difficulty. They showed that the inhabitants had a primitive life. However, the Captain was very excited to see the utensils. They signified life. Technology had not touched Kepler-438b yet. If they would survive, they could offer technology to Kepler-438b faster than they had offered it to the earth.

After receiving the Doctor's short autopsy report and the Co-pilot's survey, the Captain looked around with his binoculars.

Captain
What are they?

Philip
What?!

Captain
Those small white shiny parts on the ground!?

Philip
Let me see!

Philip looked carefully at the direction that the Captain pointed to.

Captain
Doctor
Co-Pilot
Allan
Andy

Philip
I don't know! Snow, salt or puddles?

Allan
Let me see!

Captain
Yes, it's not clear. Let's go there now.

Philip
But that's too far away. It's getting dark, and the crowd are waiting for us over there.

Captain
Right! Allan and the Co-pilot spend the night here. The Doctor, Philip, Andy and I will join the other passengers and spend the night with them. Tomorrow, we'll join you, and after accommodating the passengers in these cabins, we'll continue our explorations. Clear?

Allan had a horrible feeling. He had been scared to death.

Allan
Why does the Captain always ignore me? It seems that he doesn't need me any longer. He has forgotten what I did for him while he had reached an impasse.

Allan did not dare to open the valves of his heart to the Co-pilot. He was a staunch fellow of the Captain, and he could inform the Captain of Allan's detestation of him. Silence is golden, he thought. However, he was overwhelmed with anger and wanted to avenge the Captain. Anyway, he had been a clever businessperson, who had managed to ruin the lives of many of his rivals, and unlike the Captain, who had spent all his life in the laboratory and library, he knew several tricks to belittle the Captain in the eyes of all passengers. Spite and fright did not let Allan close his eyes even for a tick.

Orbit 3

Pueblos > Ademia

The daylight replaced darkness with whiteness. The Captain and the hopeful excited crowd set off for their new land and arrived there sound and safe. Allan had no idea what the Captain had said to the crowd in his absence. Perhaps he had introduced himself as a Deus ex Machina, offering survival to them. Perhaps he had told them that he had built pueblos and found water for them. Allan cast a glance at the Captain's face. He looked the happiest.

Captain
Welcome all! Here you go! Enough pueblos for now, but we have to build some more and even better ones as soon as we settle down. The color of soil as I told you is rich, and we hope to find water for you today. Now, the team leaders continue checking all cabins one by one, and then, we use the cabins.

The Captain then pointed to the gunmen and commanded them to enter the cabins and check them for safety issues. Allan who was scared to death to enter and inspect the cabins just stayed at the cabins' entrance for a while without inspecting their interiors. At the same time, the Captain walked around with pride and joy and double-checked the biggest cabin, which had been built higher than other ones. As soon as the inspection was over, the Captain addressed the whole crowd:

Captain
Alright! Due to the limited number of pueblos, every seven people
will cohabit in one cabin.

Allan
How about you?

Captain
I will take that one.

He then pointed to the biggest cabin. He then added:

Captain
The team leaders also need more space, so every three team leaders will get one cabin.

Allan
Andy
Doctor

Philip
Co-pilot
Alex

Captain
Soon we will build some more cabins, and you will have more
space. Just be patient! The fruit of patience is sweet. Now before
you enter the cabins, let me name our first land, too. As you might
know, my name is *Adam*, so let's name here *Ademia*. OK?

All people cheered up. They had become settlers with a nation

state, named Ademia. To do so, they had done ethnic cleansing by

murdering or removing the aliens from their homeland. No one

knew what had happened to those natives who managed to escape

the death scene. Few settlers sympathized for aliens; however,

many others believed that they had occupied the lands that the settlers wanted for their survival, and what was more important than survival? Allan also pre10ded to be happy. He was thinking about the new class formation. With his intelligence, he had managed to elevate his class from the third one to the second; however, he was not con10ted with his class yet.

Captain
Don't worry about the aliens. We'll teach them our own language, help them embrace our rites and respect our rights. This way they can work for us, and in return, we'll provide them with some food, but for now I think we need to find water. Allan and Andy!

Andy
Yes!

Captain
Stay here to take care of our people, and we will continue our exploration.

Doctor
Philip
Co-pilot
Alex
Allan

Unlike Andy, Allan was upset. He didn't want to stay with the settlers. Rather, he wished to set off for water exploration. He felt that the Captain favored Philip and Alex more than him and Andy. He was also curious to learn about the white spots that the Captain and Philip had detected with the binoculars. If water, the Captain would be known as the saviour, so Allan wished for the Captain's fiasco.

The closer the Captain and his comrades got to the intended site, the more stressed they became. What if what they had seen were salt or lime? What if they were mirage?

Captain
There might be something here; otherwise, aliens would have not nested here.

Alex
True!

Philip
That is great that we have guns. Otherwise, how could we protect ourselves against these queer animals?

Alex
Animals!

Philip
They are neither plants nor human beings. What else could they be?

Alex
Humanimals or angels!

Philip
How about freaks? If we could go back to the earth, we could take some of them and exhibit them. This could attract curious peoples and their money.

Alex
Alex
Alex

Earlier than expected, the Captain and his comrades reached the first white spot. Since it had been located after a small hill, they had not even seen this one with the binoculars.

92

Captain
Doctor, what's that?

Doctor
Let me zee!

Captain
Philip
Alex
Co-pilot

The Doctor knelt down and probed the spot. It was a small puddle, containing some colorless liquid. The Doctor smelled it. It smelled unpleasant. He   sit   ant   ly, he tasted it. Everyone was waiting for the Doctor to notify them of the result of his probe.

Doctor
Mmm, I'm not zure, but . . .

Captain
But what?

Doctor
Thiz liquid boz zmellz and taztez like ammonia, and it'z not drinkable!

Captain
Oh no! What shall we do?

Alex
Perhaps aliens have dissolved ammonia in it to avenge us!

Captain
What do you think, Doctor?

Doctor
I zuggezt that we ezamine ozer nearby puddlez.

Captain
I agree!

The closer they got to other puddles, the yellower the land became. They could even detect some molds. To the Doctor, those species of fungi grew in areas with high humidity. That was a good and bad news. It signified the existence of moisture, while at the same time the yellow spongy molds signified health problems, since many molds, as the Doctor described, were common allergens that could cause severe respiratory disorders. The poisonous chemicals, so-called mycotoxins, could cause other serious long-term asthma, migraines, rashes, pneumonia, hives, sinus infections, extreme fatigue and joint inflammation.

These words milled all hopes growing in the hearts of the Captain and his fellows - - - - - - - - - -

Captain
So how can we get rid of these species?

Doctor
Moldz penetrate into materialz, and it'z really hard to remove or eradicate them.

Captain
Forget about cleansing molds now. So the presence of these molds means that the water in other puddles contain ammonia, too!

Doctor
I'm not zure!

Captain
So let's examine them, too!

The Doctor probed the other puddles one by one. All puddles both smelled and tasted ammonia!

Captain
As you all know, our water storage is scarce, and if we fail to find water, we'll ...

The utterance of this incomplete remark worsened the headache of the Captain; the headache that had nested in his head since he had removed his oxygen mask. He squeezed his eyes and pressed his forehead with his fingers so hard that it left a deep imprint on his forehead.

Doctor
To me, it'z quite natural. We should not ezpect to find the zame water that we uzed on the earz. Az we have a different air quality here, we have a different water quality juzt like yellow moldz instead of green onez.

Captain
But this water is not potable!

Doctor
Zere are plenty of puddlez here, and zey might be different in type juzt like uz.

The Doctor continued examining other puddles. Some of them were tepid, while some were cold; some were small, while some were big; some smelled more, while some smelled less. The Doctor drank little water from a puddle that smelled the least.

Captain
How do you feel?

Doctor
Horrible!

The Doctor's statement made all worried!

Captain
What do you mean?

Doctor
I feel zick! I wanna . . .

The Doctor then squeezed his belly with his hands and puked his guts out. However, since he had not eaten anything for long, he just threw up some thick sticky saliva. To wash away his shame and saliva, he sat down and washed his face with water from the same puddle.

The Captain and his fellows were nervous and helpless. In a few moments, something strange started to happen. The Doctor's eyebrows and long beard which he had not shaved after departure started to fall out in clumps! His skin also became red and itchy.

Captain
Oh my gosh!

Philip
The water is more corrosive and aggressive than we thought!

The Captain looked around with his binoculars.

Captain
These puddles are everywhere.

Philip
Do the aliens drink the same venom?

Alex
I think so! That's why they're all bald.

Philip
So what do they eat?

Alex
Good question!

The Doctor was suffering from bellyache. Everyone looked disappointed. The Captain sat down on the ground, thinking what would happen if they lose the Doctor. He was thirsty and exhausted, but he had to keep his spirits up; otherwise, the others would not think of him as the commander-in-chief. He suddenly stood up.

Captain
No worries at all! We have water for a while, and I'm confident that we will find water before our supply gets over.

Philip
Really!? But just a few moments ago you said that our storage is scarce!

The Captain walked away, and the other gunmen followed him. The Doctor also tried to join them, but he felt so faint that he leaned against a rock to save himself from falling. The Captain suddenly stopped. It was clear like day that his words had failed to inflate his comrades. He looked around with his binocular, but there were no signs of life!

With his bald and pale face, the Doctor was no longer a familiar figure.

How Soon!

How soon everything might change

and familiar becomes eeestrangeee

How soon it becomes late

and changes our destined fate

How soon days and nights pass

and we break like a piece of glass

How soon!

Soon they reached a hill. They climbed it with difficulty, step-by-step, gasping. They at.tempted to mush their way through the jumbles of rocks. They frequently sat down to take some rest and remove the pebbles from their shoes. This had slowed down and in some cases halted their moves. They envied their fellows who stayed in the aliens' abandoned abject abodes.

Eventually, the Captain accelerated up the hill, and he was panting when he re.ached the top. He was ex.cited to see what was down the h.ill; however, he was mel.led with a sense of fear and hope, a sense of duality and indeterminacy, joy and sorrow, hope and despair. He was on the edge, but this feeling did not last long. Soon a relieved sigh came as he perceived the other side of the edge. He could not believe his eyes! He rubbed his eyes and lOOked again.

Captain
Oh my God! Come on, come on!

Alex
Why?

Captain
Come and see with your own eyes!

The gunmen, except the Doctor who was still sick, hurried up. Like the Captain, they did not believe their eyes! The scenery had inspired them with life and joy. They could see some yellow pastures and a river with naked eye. Life had shown its beautiful side to them. They ran down the hill. Several times, they fell and rolled down the hill, but heedlessly, they stood up again and ran down the steep hill. Before long, they arrived down there, and after they smelled no rat, they happily jumped into the river. To remove their thirst, they drank as much as they really wished. What a relief or rather a re.life!

Captain
Didn't I tell you that I'll find water? Here you go!

They all cheered up! Alex jumped up and down. The Captain tightly hugged Philip.

Survivance
    Existence
        Subsistance
Permanence
    Abidance
        Continuance

Their happiness, however, did not last long. Before long, they all got sick! They were all lying on the ground, puking their guts out. They also lost all their body hair. Their skins were reddish, too. They looked like white-skinned hairless cats!

Captain
But . . . it didn't . . . s.mell!

Alex
Right . . . we were . . . de.ceived by the . . . pastures baaaarf

Philip
Sometimes . . . . those that . . . don't smell . . . are more . . . hazardous.

While holding their bellies and throwing up all their joys with grief, they looked around.

Captain
But . . . if it contained . . . ammonia, how have these plants grown!?

Philip
Perhaps . . . baarf . . . they are used to it! Barrrf

Captain
Oh no! My stom.ache is . . . . baaarf . . .in my mouth. Will . . . we get . . . used to it?

Alex
No way! When it . . . does this to our hair . . . . . and skin, what does it do . . . with our stomache?! Baaaaaarf

Philip
Oh no! We are all bald!

They were all sad. The Captain stood up and moved toward the pasture. He then knelt down, picked a weed and smelled it. Is there any cattle here? Has anybody planted them? Does it rain here? The Captain had many questions, but the ache was killing him. He pressed his belly repeatedly. Suddenly, he lied down. He could feel death. At this time, the Doctor who dragged himself with difficulty joined them, but he was unable to help anyone. He could not help even himself. He sat down on the ground, grabbed the binoculars and lOOked around. After all, he had a better feeling compared to his companions. To his great surprise, he detected some moving objects in distant. He fOcused on them. However, he had no idea what they were!

Doctor
Zomzing iz moving, zomzing iz moving! Come and zee.

These words made everyone vigilant. The Captain dragged himself toward the Doctor and grabbed the binoculars.

The Doctor was right. Something was moving over there. The moving objects made the gunmen forget about their ache. Then, they decided to move closer to the moving objects.

Soon they found that they were aliens. Now the gunmen were sure that the pastures belonged to the aliens. If so, perhaps they raised some cattle and fowl. Perhaps they grew different crops. Perhaps they had some better water to drink.

They approached the aliens, and the Captain observed them with his binoculars:

Captain

I see about 10 aliens . . . two of them are sitting . . . and the others are working . . . . Some carry straws . . . . and some are hand-picking some crops.

Then, he stopped reporting and asked his men to lis10 at10tively to his plan.

Captain

Look! Now they are within our shooting range, but I suggest to get as close as possible, and then we open fire. It seems that they have some better dwellings here, much better than what we occupied yesterday.

Doctor

But . . . but zey are defenzelez. Perhapz we can talk to zem.

Alex

Talk to them?! In what language? I suggest that we capture and use them as working hands. Free labor!

Captain

No way! They might counter-attack us. Under.stand?!

Alex

Now we all look like each other: bald bods and red skins. Instead of attacking them, we approach them and . . .

Captain

I cannot imagine cohabiting with these weird and sickening crea-tures even for a tick. So let's move closer and then open fire.

Alex

But let's observe what they do. Perhaps we learn the secrets of life on Kepler-438b.

Captain

Enough is enough! It's no time for observation, so shake a leg!

The Captain looked at the aliens one more time and quickly reviewed his plan in his mind. There were about ten aliens working outside, but the number of dwellings showed that there would be more than ten aliens living in that re.side.nce. Where are the other ones? Are they working in.side or in distant areas and return by dusk? He whispered while keeping them under surveil.lance. All of a sudden, they heard a banshee scream right behind their heads. The loud scream made them up shooting aimlessly at different directions. This made the aliens escape the scene. In spite of this, the Captain and his gunmen managed to murder three aliens. Then, they moved toward the dwellings while shooting. This made some aliens scared, leaving their abiding places hurriedly, and this increased the number of casualties. Altogether they murdered ten aliens.

Soon the Captain asked the Co-pilot and Alex to investigate inside the dwellings. Their cabins, which had been built on the ground, were lighter and more spacious than the previous ones, located in a dry area. The new aliens also seemed to be more civilized, since they had some better cooking utensils and farming tools.

While Alex and the Co-pilot were inside, the Captain and the Doctor were probing the water of lakes. The Doctor tasted one of them and got sick again for a while, but the level of his sickness was not as harsh as it was before.

Captain
Does the water contain less ammonia, or are you getting used to it?

Doctor
No idea! Perhapz I'm getting uzed to it, juzt like ze air.

Captain
Right! Once a boy living in a poor household asked his dad, "How long our poverty lasts?" His dad answered, "For 40 days." The son happily asked, "so we get rid of poverty after 40 days?" and his dad retorted, "No, we just get used to it!"

Doctor
Doctor
Doctor

After probing the water quality, they walked toward the aliens' dead bodies. The Captain had no he.art to approach them, so he surv.eyed them from far away. The Doctor, however, got closer and examined them one by one. Some of them had yellowish blood, while a couple of them had purple blood. It was strange, the Doctor thought! What is the mystery behind different blood colors?

He examined their bodies carefully. Those aliens with purple blood were sturdy and had softer skins, while the yellow-blooded aliens were skinnier with harsh skins. Perhaps the yellow-blooded aliens were laborers toiling for the ones with purple blood, he pondered.

Orbit 2

D.well.ing

They had a horrible night. In fact, they were either fully awake patrolling around the dwellings or traumatically awake rolling side to side. They could not sleep where aliens used to sleep. How could they sleep on beds whereon aliens had slept? In fact, the aliens had no real beds. They had raised the ground level with clay and had spread some soft dry soil all over to make it cozy. They had no pillows, and in lieu of blankets, they used some plants knitted together. Alex could detect some crochet patterns in his blanket. Despite this very basic life, this dwelling, compared to the former one, looked more "modern!"

Alex
I suppose aliens here also have the first and third worlds! These ones living here are the first world aliens.

Philip
Hahaha! Good observation. Di.vi.si.on.s always exist! Alex, do you know what I'm thinking about?

Alex
You are thinking about your luxury life on the earth, or perhaps you have missed your maids and secretaries. Now I know! You are thinking about the aliens, which you have killed, or the ones that managed to escape and now are out of their dwellings.

Philip had no idea how many aliens he had killed after setting foot on Kepler-438b, but he had turned into a murderer! After a long pause, Philip went on:

Philip
I wish I was an ordinary third class settler with no gun!

Early in the morning, the Captain and the Doctor continued their examinations, and soon they informed others that the quality of water in a well, located in the northern side of their dwelling place is much better. The gunmen, except the Captain, drank some water. The Captain wanted to see what happens to his servicemen. He observed their awful sickness with care; however, their sickness did not last long.

Captain
How do you feel this time?

Alex
Sickness k.ills.

Doctor
But ziz time it iz much better, izn't it?!

Alex
Philip
Co-pilot

The gunmen had a mixed feeling. They didn't know to feel happy or sad. They were happy, since they had eventually found "water," which was less sickening, but sad, since they had lost all their hair and had been left with a red itchy skin!

Then, they looked around with care. After a while, they came across a huge cabin, located on the other side of the d.well.ings. Its door had been b.locked with some straws.

Captain
What is there?

Alex
Aliens, I think.

Doctor
Lizen! I hear a ztrange zound!

Alex
A strange sound?!

All of a sudden, Alex, who looked terrified, started shooting at the cabin from where he was. Suddenly a huge weird creature got out of the cabin, and Alex shot it. The poor creature laid on the ground, and blood sprayed out of its wounds. They witnessed its last agony. It was not an alien, but a bizarre animal with no fur.

Alex remembered his own memories of bow hunting during weekends in fall. He remembered how joyful it was when he and his companies furtively approached a deer, drew and released an arrow and hit the deer. He always enjoyed watching and recording the last moments of deer's agony; however, due to some harsh criticism he received, he did not dare to share them on his social media.

The Captain asked the Co-pilot and Alex to enter the cabin and find about the source of the strange sounds, which had increased.

Alex had been scared to death. He looked pale, believing that what he had done to poor animals and aliens would return to him after entering the cabin.

Alex
I think it's the Doctor's turn.

Captain
Stop foolishness and get in. We have only one Doctor here.

Alex
How about Philip? It's his turn after all, isn't it?

Philip, who did not expect such a reaction from his fellow, frowned at Alex, and with a heavy sigh, he followed the Co-pilot. Upon entering, they were surprised. It was not a cabin but a barn. They could see some weird creatures of different sizes. Some of them looked like the one that Alex had killed, while some others looked like birds with red skins with no feather. In a small coop, built in the barn's corner, the Co-pilot found some tiny yellow eggs. It seemed that the poor aliens were skilled farmers, who also raised some animals and birds.

Philip
We wiped them out and occupied their lands, farms, barns and coops. Our ancestors did the same to Native Ame…

Philip's words were interrupted by some gunshots. They hurriedly got out of the barn and saw the gunmen running toward some aliens and shooting at them. They joined their fellows, shooting toward some aliens that had come very close to their dwellings, throwing spears and arrows toward the Captain and his fellows.

They had returned to get their lands back, but it was a futile effort. Many more lost their lives in the battle, while some others fled after perceiving their fellows falling off like red leaves in the fall.

The Captain attempted to chase the runaway ones to kill some more, but he was too dazed to rush. He felt a sudden pain in his right leg, and when he looked down, he found that he had been injured. It seemed that one of the arrows had struck his leg, and it was bleeding. Immediately, he lied on the ground, calling the Doctor to help him, while his face was distorted with rage.

Captain
I will avenge on you, ugly creatures! You'll see!

Doctor
Calm down! It'z not zeriouz.

Captain
Nothing serious? Open your eyes! I'm bleeding!

Doctor
Alex
Co-pilot
Philip

Silence reigned for a while. The Captain, who was guilty of conscious for shouting at the Doctor, attempted to break the silence.

Captain
Philip, what did you find inside?

Philip
Philip
Philip

Captain
Hey, I'm talking to you!

Philip
It's a . . . barn. There are several animals of different types and sizes.

Captain
Really?! Wow, what could be better than this?! Thank you for the great news. Let's go and see!

The Captain stood up and walked like a lame lamb toward the barn.

Captain
Watch here while the Doctor and I visit the barn. Are the animals tame?

Philip
I think so!

The Captain held the hand of the Doctor and entered the barn. He looked excited. That was unbelievable to him who always believed that aliens were fictitious. Now he could see them with his own eyes; however, they could not have anything like UFOs! They were so primitive!

Captain
Look, from now on, we also have some animals to ride, some eggs and m.eat to eat, some water to drink and some places to dwell. We have our own colony. We survived, we survived!

His cheers encouraged the Co-pilot, Philip and Alex to enter the barn.

110

Philip
What's going on here?

Captain
What's going on here?! Life! Look! We survived.

The Doctor also looked impressed. He went to the cOOp and grabbed one of the eggs. It was still warm. Then, he hit it against a wall. It broke and a gelatin sticky grey liquid splashed on the wall. This frightened all the cattle and birds and made them scream, screech and squeal.

Philip
Yes, YEs, YES! It's life, but why is it grey? Life has a different color here, doesn't it?

Captain
Now, it's time to see if we can ride these chargers. Let's take one of them out. Look over there! There are some saddles and devices used by aliens for riding them. They are too basic, but we improve them as soon as we settle down. Co-pilot, take this one out. That one, I mean the small one. It's always good to start with the small ones. They are easier to control.

The Co-pilot attempted to hold and move a small red-skinned charger out. The Captain then asked Alex to fetch a saddle and some cords and attach them to the submissive charger. Its long neck had made the job more demanding. Their lack of experience in installing the devices on it made the charger turbulent after a while, making the job even harder than it was. The Doctor suggested moving the charger toward the water hole to pacify it. Upon seeing the water, it moved its head down and lapped it up.

While it was busy lapping up the water, they put the devices on it.
Soon it was ready for the Captain to try it. He mounted on it, and it
was joyful. The animal was obedient, and it was easy to control it.
It seemed that the aliens had well trained them.

Captain
How many of them do we have?

Doctor
zeven, I think.

Captain
Great. Seven gunmen, seven chargers. The equation works.

He then rode the charger around. His grin revealed his joy. The
charger was not that fast, but it could facilitate and accelerate their
investigations.

Captain
It's wonderful! I'll come back in a minute.

Philip
Take care!

The Captain tried the charger for a while around the dwellings.
Then, he suddenly stopped and dismounted *his* charger.

Captain
Now it's time to transfer others from the old dwelling site to here.
The Doctor and I keep watch over here. Alex and the Co-pilot will
go there and move them here. OK?

Alex
What?! Me? Oh no! I'm dead tired. Thinking about the h.ill that I
have to mount makes me ill.

Captain
This is the second time that in one single day you are disobeying
me. This is not tolerable.

Alex
Alex
Alex

The Captain's reaction made Philip laugh in his heart.
Captain
You don't need to walk or climb the hill. Just enjoy riding one of
these chargers. Do you under.stand me?

Alex
OK, but let us sleep over here tonight and de.part in the morning.

Captain
Fine!

Alex
And since we will be on the way tomorrow, please exempt us from
patrolling tonight. OK?

The Captain sighed!

Captain
OK. What else!?

Alex
Nothing.

Captain
So let's go and choose two chargers for you!

They all walked toward the barn. The Captain entered first and
chose two medium-sized chargers for Alex and the Co-pilot. Then,
they tried to make them ready for riding tests. Alex had hunted

many animals, but he had never ridden one. He was distressed. What if they go berserk?!

After some struggle, the Doctor helped Alex into the saddle. He grabbed the saddle horn, pulled himself up and mounted the charger! He took a deep breath.

Alex
Holy cow! How high I am.

Captain
Ride around carefully. You have a long way to ride, so you should be prepared.

Alex
Let's find a name for them.

Captain
Let's call them "hoarse."

Alex rode at an easy trot. He was more than cautious. What could he do if his hoarse went mad and broke into a furious gallop?

After the riding test, they collected some eggs at the Captain's behest. Then, the Captain, the Doctor, the Co-pilot, Philip and Alex sat around the water hole and started eating them raw. They tasted awful! The Captain threw them up right after swallowing them. The other settlers had the same feeling but tried to resist. They thought that the raw eggs were more nutritious and natural than the capsules. The Captain then informed his men that he had some tools such as matches in the spaceship, which would help them make fire and cook their food. He also promised to contact

NASA and ask them to send some other necessary stuff for their more convenient lives if any NASA still existed. His words cherished dreams of a better life in all.

Early in the morning, Alex and the Co-pilot departed. It was the first night that Alex had a short but full-time sleep. In his sweet dreams, he had seen how he was building his own skyscrapers on Kepler-438b.

After climbing and descending the hill, the journey became boring. It was a flat wasteland, a land of death! They had got some water plus some grass for chargers and some eggs for themselves. It was even more boring for Alex to travel with the Co-pilot, who was laconic. He used his head instead of his tongue in communications and always nodded.

Alex
Why doesn't he move his small tongue instead of his big head?!

After a dull day, they arrived|alived to the intended site. As soon as Alex saw the settlers, he called them out. All of a sudden, Allan and Andy opened fire on Alex and the Co-pilot. The strident sound shot fear throughout the Co-pilot's and Alex's h.ear.ts. Alex yelled and attempted to introduce himself, but the earsplitting sound of shooting did not let them hear Alex. Desperately, Alex started shooting into the sky to signal who they are, but this made the situation even worse, making Allan and Andy shoot in a frenzy.

Since they were hairless and were riding some strange animals, Allan and Andy had mistaken them for aliens. To defend themselves, Alex and the Co-pilot shot back, and in a few moments, Allan was shot in the chest. Immediately, Andy put down his gun and surrendered. Soon it was revealed that some bullets had hit one of the chargers. The poor animal suddenly sat down on its haunches. It was bleeding.

Alex and the Co-pilot rushed toward Allan.

Alex
Andy, give me a hand.

Andy
Andy?! What?! Who are you?

Alex
Who am I?! I'm Alex. Why did you open fire on us? Had you lost it?

Andy sighed!

Andy
Alex, what has happened to you?! You look like aliens! Why have you changed so much?

Alex pretended that he hadn't heard him. A swift survey sufficed to find that Allan had lost his life. It was a tragic scene. How could he kill his fe.ll.ow?! Alex cried his heart out. The Co-pilot and Andy attempted to make him simmer down, but they failed. Tears rolled down their faces, too.

Sadly, they held a quick funeral ceremony for Allan. In fact, he had lost his life to protect his people. They made a tomb for him. In his brief speech that made everyone cry, Alex praised Allan's bravery, calling him a warrior, who devoted his life for his own people.

Right after the funeral, they all returned to their cabins. Alex and the Co-pilot spent the night there and notified Andy of the new d.well.ing they had found. Since Andy was curious to learn more about their new dwelling, he bombarded them with his questions. They all had totally forgotten Allan and his death.

Early in the morning, Andy gathered all residents and informed them of their migration. He exaggerated about the new dwelling in his speech, and unlike the Co-pilot, Alex looked contented. People cheered up as if they were going to move to a paradise, as if Allan had not been killed, as if all their pains had been healed, as if all their miseries had terminated. However, all the settlers had one big question which no one dared to ask: If the new dwelling is so great, why Alex and the Co-pilot had lost all their hair? Would this happen to them?!

The Co-pilot, who had emigrated in his youth from a third-world country to the US in search of a better life and had faced lots of dis.crime.nations, could foresee the frustration and disappointment in the faces of people soon after entering their new accommodation!

Alex asked all to take whatever they had found handy in their cabins. Now, they had only one charger, and a lot of stuff to carry. To facilitate their move, they attempted to load some of their bigger and heavier stuff on the charger. Soon the migration started.

The Co-pilot was fully aware of the hardships of the migration ahead; however, the false promises pumped up by Alex in migrants had kept them on their toes.

Orbit 1

Slave Ship

It was dusk when they arrived on top of the hill. Alex, Andy and the Co-pilot were worried that the Captain, Philip and the Doctor think of them as aliens and open fire on them. They had been baptised with fire just yesterday, and they didn't wish to be re-baptized! Alex and Andy had different views. Alex believed that they would shoot to warn them of their presence, and then they all move together, while Philip believed that it would be safer to pass the night over the hill and arrive there in the morning light.

After some arguments, they decided to pass the night out and move toward the new residential area together in the morning, shout and shoot on the way to notify the settlers of their arrival. They had hard times sleeping out. Like many of his companions, the Co-pilot could not close his eyes, thinking that they might be attacked at any moment by the aliens. After a short while, the Co-pilot started walking around and reviewing his life hi.story; his childhood, how he escaped death from a genocide that happened in his teenage, how he moved to the US without his parents to study, how he was mistreated due to his race and how the mistreatments that he received negatively affected his self-confidence. He sighed! Despite all his successes in his studies, research findings, missions and jobs, he had to serve under the Captain, who . . . . He decided not to think about it. The more he thought about the past, the more he suffered!

Early in the morning, they set off for their new "home." They were all dead tired, but as agreed, they made some noises, and their strident noises and voices alerted the Captain, Philip and the Doctor of their fellowmen's arrival. They hugged the migrants as if they had not met for ten light years! The Captain and the Doctor accommodated the settlers based on their arrangements. They had also selected two spacious cabins for themselves. The settlers were curious to learn about their new environment, so they moved around and tried to discover as much as they could. They could somehow feel the differences between the new and old cabins, but there was a huge difference between what they expected and what they witnessed.

Captain
Alex, move the chargers to the barn and feed them.

Alex
OK!

The Captain did not notice that Allan and one of the chargers are missing, and Alex wished to keep everything dark. Before long, they fell asleep, and silence reigned. Andy was perplexed why the Captain, Philip and the Doctor did not even ask about Allan. How worthless man has become, Andy thought!

Man's worthless
Comes and goes! Death.
No one cares!

He jumps stairs
To sit on chairs! Death.
Nonsense, nonsense!

He errs and errs
Loses hairs! Death.
No offense!

At about noontime, people got up one after the other and left their cabins. Their presence made the site noisy, but some contradictions between what they had heard from Alex and what they could see with their own eyes made it noisier. The Captain soon appeared and asked about the reasons for their kerfuffle.

To make them silent, the Captain made a long speech. In his speech, he noted how *he* had made them escape the earth before its death, how *he* had helped them get rid of their oxygen cylinders, how *he* had exterminated aliens, how *he* had offered his fellows residence and how *he* had found water for them. Then, *he* made some promises, assuring that *he* is not contented with what he had already achieved and that *he* would do his best to make their life cosier! His words brought back silence and optimism to the crowd.

During the Captain's speech, the Co-pilot was thinking how the Captain ignored all other people's services and recorded everything as his own accomplishments. This is the nature of life. Many people work, but one, who is on top, always gets the credits.

Then, the Captain asked everyone to collaborate in order to improve the conditions of their residential area, plantations and livestock. They also had to build some more places to facilitate life for those who had been packed in one tiny cabin. However, none of those people had been a working hand, and that had slowed down their progress.

The Captain and his gunmen searched around the dwelling every day to see whether they can find anything new. They had found some bushes with some tropical fruits. They had also found some plants with some seeds that they ground and drank, but they had a long distance to attain their dreams. Eventually, the Captain decided to go to the spaceship to both collect some of the necessary stuff they had left there and contact NASA.

One day, the Captain, the Doctor and the Co-pilot mounted their chargers and set off for the spaceship. They asked other gunmen to guard the area until they are back. The poor condition of the air, water and nutrition had made them feeble, but they had no choice. On the way, the Captain opened his heart to his fellows:

Captain
As you know, none of us has been made for such a harsh life. We cannot expect these billionaires to work like laborers. We have two options: one, to catch some aliens and force them to work for us, and two, to ask the people in NASA to send us some working hands.

Captain
Captain
Captain

After a hiatus, the Captain went on:

Captain
I think it's hard to catch and tame aliens if any left, so we have only one option.

Doctor
Are you zeriouz?!

Captain
YES! Do you have any better idea? Do you think we can survive with these lazy bones here?

Doctor
No, but I doubt the feazibility of your plan.

Captain
Let's see!

After a long way, they arrived to the spaceship. It was getting dark. The chargers had made their journey faster and easier, but all of the gunmen had some great pains on their back and between their legs. They entered the spaceship and packed some of the equipment they really needed. Then, the Captain switched on the transmitter.

Captain
Hello, this is 438b, 438b. Do you hear me? This is the Captain speaking. Do you hear me?

Co-pilot
Doctor

Captain
This is 438b, 438b. This is the Captain speaking. Do you hear me? Do you hear me?

Doctor
Captain
Co-pilot

Captain
Do you hear me? Please reply if you hear me.

Doctor
Captain

NASA
YES, we hear you. Are you okay?

Captain
Yes!

NASA
Great to hear that you are fine. Why didn't you contact us earlier?

Captain
We were engaged with the exploration operation.

NASA
Brief us. Many people are here to hear from you.

Captain
True. Hard life we have, hard life.

The Captain gave a brief report from the time they had left the spaceship, the number of casualties, the aliens, the air and water poor quality, cabins, lack of proper food, livestock, etc. He also asked for some working hands to be sent to Kepler-438b.

NASA
I'll transfer your message to the administer and deputy administer of NASA. I'll reply as soon as I hear from them.

Captain
How long would it take?

NASA
I'll reply back in a few hours. Now I send our recorded communication to them. They have been waiting too long for it, and I'm confident that they'll be so excited to hear that you are sound and safe.

Captain
Great. I'll keep the transmitter on, waiting for your message.

The Captain asked the Co-pilot and the Doctor to collect and pack some more stuff. He sat down right in front of the transmitter, waiting for a response from NASA.

Doctor
It'z funny zat zey zink we are zound and zafe here! I waz an immigrant to ze UZ. Ziz iz what uzually zoz in your homeland zink about zoz who immigrate! Zey zink of zem az a carefree pro-zperouz wiz no ztrez.

The Co-pilot nodded.

We die here; they sup.pose we are sound!

We wound here; they presume we're crowned!

We feel sick here; they feel we fool around!

We lose hair here; they hear our hair abound!

The Co-pilot nodded again.

NASA
Captain, Captain, do you hear me?

Captain
YES, YES!

NASA
The administer, his deputy and their advisory team listened carefully to your words. They wanted me to tell you that they are very happy to hear that you have settled down. They need some more time to review your request, so bear with us.

Captain
Please note that our water and food supply are limited on the spaceship, so we appreciate it if you reply as soon as possible.

NASA
Roger.

The gunmen spent the night in the spaceship. They had a good night sleep. Early in the morning, they ate some eggs and then fed the chargers. They had matches but no dry plant or grass to make a fire and cook their eggs. Always something lacks. You have eggs and grass but no matches; you have eggs and matches but no grass!

They had a dull day, a long day with nothing to do.

NASA
Captain, Captain, do you hear me?

Captain
YES, YES!

NASA
The administer agreed to send you some working hands. However, it takes some time to prepare and modify a spaceship for that purpose and to collect and dispatch some laborers.

Captain
Really?! Thanks! By the way, how is the situation on the earth?

NASA
It's getting more horrible day by day! Good for you that left here!
We all envy you!

Captain
Really?!

NASA
Yes! I hope we join you before the death of the earth.

Captain
I understand. So we well prepare Kepler for your arrival. Anyway,
I visit the spaceship after a while to learn about the laborers' dis-
patch process.

NASA
Roger!

The Captain, the Co-pilot and the Doctor felt relieved. The working hands could facilitate life for them just like the slaves who
facilitated the life of American plantation owners.

Soon, those in NASA enticed some poor wo.men as indentured
servants to escape the earth, filled with filth and death, and move
to Kepler-438b. Under promises of peace and prosperity, two hundred people, affected by Kepler Fever, bid farewell to the earth.
Life on Kepler-438b had become the dream of many earthly people, and these poor workers were happy that life was finally show-
ing its happy face to them.

Captain
200 hundred people in one spaceship?!

Co-pilot
Doctor

NASA
Yes! We are aware of the space limitation in the spaceship, but no choice. So the more, the better. It's economical. Moreover, we're sure you and the upcoming settlers would need them.

Co-pilot
Doctor
Captain

Captain
200 hundred working hands by one spaceship.

Doctor
We were only one hundred pazengerz in one zpazip and fazed many problemz. Remember? Are zey zending uz working men or Guinea men? Iz zat a zpazip or zlave zip?

The Captain was carefree. What he cared for the most was his own power, position, privilege, prosperity and property!

To transport as many as working wo.men as possible, NASA made the seats smaller and the space between the seat rows tighter. To open space for more seats, they also removed the sport facilities. Soon they dispatched two hundred working hands along with some tools and seeds, as requested by the Captain, to Kepler-438b. Due to the crammed conditions, the poor passengers had little or no room to move. They had to remain seated during the whole trip. Their abhorrent life conditions led to a high mortality rate, and about one third lost their lives in passage between the earth and Kepler-438b. The others were not sure to pass the Middle P.ass.age and see the New Promised World. They were furious with their decision for relocation.

After a fatal journey, some of them finally landed on Kepler-438b. The Captain and his crew forced the newcomers to get used to the new harsh environment with no introduction and preparation. They forced them to remove their oxygen masks and breathe without oxygen cylinders and drink the toxic water. The Captain also decided to settle them in the former dwelling site of the aliens. The newcomers had to walk a long way every day to the plantations, work there for the whole day and then return to their dwellings in the evening. They started cultivating certain vital crops such as rice, wheat and cotton. They also were forced to make new farmlands and houses for their landlords. Soon, they found that their dreams were not interpreted, and although they underwent mental agony and physical suffering, they just advanced the welfare of their masters. Instead of salary, they received some small portion of food and water, and thus, they were always hungry and thirsty.

Soon, the property owners had their own premises. They married and had children, while they held relationship with their maids. Some proprietors then managed to explore some mines. Some others started exploring and refining water in different areas, and that helped them to expand their territories. To earn more lands, they also murdered more aliens. Some of the aliens who managed to escape massacre later died of smallpox, a disease brought to Kepler-438b by the "P.ill.grims."

The good news of the settlers' survival and success made some more passengers to immigrate to Kepler-438b in different classes.

Those who immigrated with their own capitals could purchase house and plantation from property owners and hired some poor immigrants to work for them in their houses and lands.

Each spaceship transferred some high-tech equipment from the earth. Bit by bit, the number of settlers grew, and their small settlements eventually grew to become town-like. Since they had man's collective knowledge behind themselves, their progress was faster than it was expected. Bit by bit, cities and states were formed, and a constitution was written by some of the main figures. Some states agreed to the Constitution; however, some others disapproved it, believing that it would provide the central government with unlimited power. Accordingly, the passage of the Constitution caused a di.vision among those who opposed federalism. The Constitution had also introduced the government as a republic, elected by the people; however, it was hard to believe that a landlord's vote and voice would be as equal and as loud as his workers'; the workers who worked for free without freedom. Some areas with vast plantations wanted to maintain the free hand working system, while some others wished to abolish it. The Constitution also caused strong disagreements over having state or central governments.

Despite that, some elections, including presidential election, were held in Ademia at different intervals. Presidential campaigns were organized, but as expected, the Captain was "elected." He called for Ademia System, spending capitals on banking, transportation and communication systems. Consequently, bigger cities, factories, railroads, telecommunication companies were built in Ademia.

Captain
Folks, I redeemed my first promise. Now Ademia is industrialized. It is modern. We have some factories. We are fast developing.

Allan
Shut your big mouth! Which factories have you built? Only clothing factories! For whom? For your favorite businessper.sons. At what costs? At the costs of exploiting some poor wo.men in exchange of some food! If I were alive, I would not let you get there!

Captain
Thanks folks! I could not get here without your support.

Allan
Fuck you! You have never got anywhere. Ademia is still a nation of poor farmers and sharecroppers.

The implementation of Ademia System pushed out many more aliens of their lands. The Captain asked for the construction of weapons factories, believing that they need protective power to stand against aliens' attacks. Accordingly, weapons were mass-produced, and armies were formed in several states. The Captain also wished to eradicate the free working hand system, holding that all citizens should enjoy equality in Ademia; however, not all states favoured his commandment. This caused some 10sions between different states, split them and kindled the fire of a civil war. The opposing states had brave and well-experienced battlefield tacticians, such as Lee Stonewall and Jack Robert, who had fought in several wars, including the World War I, II and III, Vietnam War, Lebanese Civil War, Cambodian Civil War, Invasion of Panama, Iraq War, American led-intervention in Libya and Syria, and had great ideas of how to win the war; however, the states that supported the Captain as their commander-in-chief had better weapons. In addition, the Captain declared the Emancipation Proclamation in the middle of the war, which supposedly ended free working hand system, and this moved the poor farmers and workers to join and fight in the Captain's army. Eventually, the Captain won the war, and free working hand system faded away on paper.

Allan
You son of a bitch! I wish I was there to teach you a lesson not to forget!

Alice
Hold on! It's good that he could free the poor working hands.

Allan
He is a man of word. Do you think he has equalized the masters and laborers?! No way! He just opened the way for the reimplementation of Jim Crow laws. Do you think the rich influential masters and landlords allow their workers to stand as equal as they are?! No, we shall expect another KKK to form. The haves will continue to exploit the have-nots but in different ways. In this equation, only the corrupt Captain abusing the political machines is the winner.

Alice
Right! History repeats itself. It is cyclical.

As freedmen, the workers found themselves free but jobless with no means to earn a living. At the same time, the landowners lacked labor force! This led to sharecropping; however, after a while, poor working conditions and high risks forced some of landless sharecroppers off the farms, seeking for jobs in factories.

Captain
Folks, I'm a firm believer in human rights. Whenever I see anyone arguing for free labor force, I feel a strong impulse to see it tried on him personally. Remember! Those who deny freedom to others deserve it not for themselves. Folks! Stand with anybody who stands rights and stands for your rights!

The crowd cheered up!

Allan
Shut your big mouth up and stop deceiving naïve people.

Some groups of people who were dissatisfied with the government's prevailing policy moved westward. Their successful discoveries made some people follow them and maintain their own realms. The enhancement of such moves resulted in the creation of new nations and formation of frontiers.

People who had come from different earthly regions named their towns and countries accordingly. Some governments were established; presidents and prime ministers were s.elected; kings and queens were crowned.

To maintain its predominance, Ademia's president called for a foreign policy, so-called "Big Stick," asking for a large and strong army, which has the power to exercise its control over *other* nations. As the most affluent and powerful nation on Kepler-438b,

Ademia attracted a steady flow of immigrants from different parts of Kepler-438b.

After the Captain, his son, the Captain Jr., who had harsher policies against immigrants, was s.elected as the new president of Ademia. Immediately, he signed the Alien Act, made it harder and longer for immigrants to enter Ademia and become its citizens. He even allowed the government to deport d.anger.ous immigrants who had even received the Ademian citizenship or those working for hostile nations. He also signed the Exclusion Act, banning the entry of some immigrants from a handful of demonized countries to Ademia.

Allan
Do you see, Alice? It is no longer a democracy, but a monarchy dressed as demo.cracy. First the father, now the son, and later the grand son!

To stop the immigration flow from its southern neighbors, the Captain Jr. ordered to build a wall, and this increased the tensions between political figures in Ademia over its budget. The president was also determined to produce some nukes to increase its power over other nations. This decision encouraged some other countries to enter a nuclear arms race with Ademia. In addition to the arms race, the Captain Jr. ordered for the establishment of Military Space Force and Space Race right after Suvia, which had emerged as a rival superpower country, launched a satellite into space, making the Ademians worried to fall behind the Suvians in the race.

Races in Races

Fight for Graces

Chase all Traces

Occupy Places

Explore Spaces

Build Arsenal Bases

Displace Faces

Races vs. Races

Races in Races

To show its power, Ademia then entered a war with Vieumia, which used to challenge the supreme authority of Ademia. Before starting the war and dispatching military forces, the Captain Jr. made a speech on TV.

Captain Jr.
I am convinced that Ademia troops with their energy, mobility and firepower can successfully smash the Vieumians in a couple of weeks.

With this assurance, Ademia's public opinion overwhelmingly supported the deployment. Though Ademia's army benefited from well-equipped soldiers commanded by well-experienced com- manders and military advisors, they failed to withstand and break the resistance and counterattacks of the Vieumians. The Suvian's support of the Vieumians was the other factor that made the war demanding and frustrating for the Ademians. Consequently, after many light years, the Ademians's troops withdrew and recorded a military failure for themselves in the history of Kepler-438b. During the war, the Ademians and the Suvians came very close to attack each other with their nukes. Their destructive rivalry resulted in the Tepid War, an indirect confrontation in different areas on Kepler-438b and an intervention in the affairs of each other and some other countries. The race between Ademia and Suvia continued, causing conflicts and wars in different countries and territories, di|vi|di|ng them, leaving so many dis   tan   ces and distresses for other settlers on Kepler-438b.

As a result, many wars recurred, and many people lost their lives. Many people were forced to leave their "homelands" to save their lives. Kepler-438b was no longer a place to live.

Orbit 10

P.ass.engers

Captain
This is your Captain speaking. Welcome to Flight 10, non-stop from Ademia to Gamma Cephei. The distance between the departure point and destination is 10 light years. Fortunately, the atmospheric condition is calm, and we are expecting a smooth and uneventful flight. Accordingly, we anticipate an on-time arrival to Gamma Cephei. The temperature in the destination is now 27 °C, which is equal to the temperature of the good olden times of Kepler-438b. Please sit back, fasten your seatbelt, relax and remember to take your nutrition capsules on time. I provide you with more information during this non-return journey. On behalf of myself and the Co-pilot, I wish you a pleasant journey.